ADOPTED

ADOPTED

THE CONTINUED STORY OF
THE WRIGHT FAMILY

CHARLES LEE KNUCKLES

PALMETTO
PUBLISHING
Charleston, SC
www.PalmettoPublishing.com

Copyright © 2024 by Charles Lee Knuckles

All rights reserved.

No portion of this book may be reproduced, stored in a retrieval system, or transmitted in any form by any means–electronic, mechanical, photocopy, recording, or other–except for brief quotations in printed reviews, without prior permission of the author.

Paperback ISBN: 979-8-8229-5709-1
eBook ISBN: 979-8-8229-5710-7

This book is dedicated to my sister Nellie Mae.

With special thanks to my friend Monte Hall even with his tireless devotion to the "Achungo Children's Center" while helping the poor children of rural Kenya, he took the time to help me with edits to this book, Adopted.

A special thanks to: CJ Fitzgerald, Justin Camp, Barney Huang, Kevin Hartley, Jozef Froniewsk, Pete Kockelman, Mark Cochran, Scott Gattey, the band of brothers that helped me retain my sanity is trying times. I don't even know if they knew it.

A special thanks to Susan Johnston who worked so hard to help me with my grammar.

A special thanks to my church family Wallingford Presbyterian Church who have adopted me and supported me through thick and thin.

Table of Contents

Little Tommy 1
The Big Bang 7
Back to School 12
Rashawn 17
Rescued by a sympathetic old gangster 24
Daydreams turn into Nightmares 29
The Truth hurts 35
It Ain't Snitching, It's The Truth! 54
Thomas Wright 67
The Adoption 74
Like Father, Like Son: Rashawn 78
The Big City and Little Tommy 84
The Great Nerd Rescue: Rashawn 91
Money Can't Call Me Honey: Tommy and Judy 96
Love: Rashawn 107
Love Would Face Tests That Only Made Love Stronger ... 115
The Wedding: Told by Tommy Wright 136
Adoption: Rashawn and Hailey 142
Tommy and Judy 163
Adopted: Tommy and Judy 166
Rashawn 182

Little Tommy

My name is Thomas Wright. I was not always a member of the Wright family--I was born Thomas O'Connor. There was a lot of shame and fear surrounding my old name. When I was adopted, I became a member of the Wright family. Now, by no small miracle, I am a pastor of a small church of a thousand members in Loren, Virginia.

Fifteen years ago, when I first left this state, I swore that I would never return. Who would have ever thought that I would fall so deeply in love with Christ Jesus that I would become a pastor? To help you understand better what I'm talking about, let me begin at the beginning.

I was born Thomas O'Connor. When I was young, I lived in, seemingly, the worst trailer park known to man. It was filled with dysfunctional families. Many were downright cruel to us kids. Certain things were just not talked about. Crime was a normal way of life.

Criminals were protected because they were the main source of income. My parents were meth-kingpins, so for the most part I was protected. I didn't have to worry about the burned-out, meth perverts in the park. Many other kids weren't so lucky. Kids in my neighborhood were groomed for crime; some for stealing, some for selling drugs and some, unfortunately, were groomed for prostitution.

They called me Little Tommy because I was so short. My parents, Tom and Beth O'Conner, groomed me to help them produce and sell their product, the deadly drug Methamphetamine. We produced meth like our trailer home was a laboratory on wheels. I was born into a family of criminals. When King David said in Psalm 51, "Behold, I was brought forth in iniquity and in sin," I get it, because it was my story from the beginning. I was conceived while my mom and pop were high on meth.

Daily, shifty characters were in and out of our home. In the process of making meth, I was in charge of lining up the ingredients for dad. I kinda think that my dad wasn't all bad. After I did my little part in the production of the meth, I think in order to protect me, he would bark the order, "Git out of here kid. Go play with your friends!"

"The danger was real, but in my parents' minds, they were using the production to survive. It was like they thought it was a legitimate business. If they would have asked me, I would have told them that their little business was a recipe for disaster, but I didn't get a vote. I was just an 11-year-old kid.

Most of us kids in that trailer park played in the streets unchaperoned. Our parents were either busy in some sort of crime or focused on getting high. I noticed that kids have a built-in desire to be kids. So, at every opportunity, we played

ADOPTED

racing each other, hide and seek, 123-Red Light, or tag. When we had the opportunity to laugh, we laughed hard, squeezing every ounce of happiness out of the moment that we could. We knew there would be other moments when we would not be able to laugh or even smile.

There was Butch, the bully. I came to realize that Butch bullied kids because his dad bullied him. Butch liked being away from his parents' trailer because his life there was often a living hell. Everybody called Ralphie, "Waldo," because he was so good at hiding. Ralphie learned the art of hiding because his so-called uncle was a bad uncle. Ralphie never spoke of the things his uncle did to him. None of us knew what was going on with Ralphie, except the sisters. The sisters, Charlotte, who everybody called Charlie, and Ruthie, knew everything that went on in the park. We all knew that by the age of ten both Charlie and Ruthie were already being marketed by their mom, but no one would dare say a word. Maybe that's why they knew about Ralphie. When the girls and Ralphie were playing with the rest of us, they could just be kids.

Our friend, Tony-No-Baloney, took no stuff off of anyone. Tony's parents were low-level members of a powerful local crime syndicate. Tony-No-Baloney, to the trailer-park residents, was like crime syndicate royalty. We often wondered why they were living in the trailer-park and the best we could figure is that someone in his family was in hiding. We never saw Tony-No-Baloney's dad, but his two older brothers would occasionally pull up in flashy cars, dressed like gangsters.

Sometimes they were with big scary guys that seemed like bodyguards.

We didn't learn much of the school curriculum. I mean, school was school, but for the greater part of our lives we were busy, mostly assessing threats that came from other kids as well as adults. I think that living on the edge of fight or flight mode aged all of us far too quickly. Some of the time, we were like adults in kids' bodies.

One time, for some reason, Butch was bullying the sisters. He was calling them names I would never repeat. That's when Tony-No-Baloney walked up to him and cracked him across the shins with a mini baseball bat. Tony kept the bat for just such occasions. We all laughed out loud at first and then snickered quietly, being careful Butch didn't hear us. I guess he couldn't hear much because he was hopping around in a dance of pain.

Tony said, "That's how my dad and my big brothers collect what's due, and what's due from you, Butch, my friend, is a little respect for the ladies."

We were all thankful that we had a compassionate thug on our side. Oh, Tony wouldn't object to that description of himself, at least not the thug part. Tony-No-Baloney wouldn't want to be seen as compassionate, but compassionate he was, especially towards those of us who he grew up with him in the park. Even if Butch could, there would be no retaliation. Butch knew that Tony's big brothers, Gianfranco and Rocco, could make him disappear at the snap of their fingers. Tony-No-Baloney had serous backup. He was a mob prince. Butch never bothered the sisters again. I think that on his bad days,

ADOPTED

when his dad was mean, Butch thought he needed to lash out on anyone he could. Tony controlled Butch's meanness by letting him know when he could and when he couldn't hurt people. He let him know that kids from the park were off-limits, especially the sisters. Tony knew that the sisters had enough misery on their plate. All of us who lived in the park had our share of problems.

Play time would be play time. It was our little vacation from the reality of the lives we had to live. Tony would keep play time safe. I guess it was also his little vacation. Although he was too cool to do certain things, like shopping cart bumping cars. He would laugh at the fun we were having, never getting too involved.

Our parents had to send us to school to keep the cops off their backs. I don't know if they would even have bothered if our absence wouldn't have drawn unwanted attention to their illegal activities. When we did go to school, although they might want to, most of the other kids were afraid to call us "trailer-park trash." Some of the older jocks were not afraid to call us names, that is, until Butch and Tony showed up. They took some kids' lunch money as a penalty for disrespecting us.

It seemed like none of us kids from the park stayed afterschool for extracurricular events. We vanished at the ring of the closing bell. We all headed home to do what we had to do for our parents.

Nobody knew what Butch's dad did for a hustle. All we knew was that he traveled in an ordinary, scary-looking van. He and Butch organized stuff in the van, but we never saw what was in the van. Our imaginations ran away with us. We would guess stuff like body parts were in the van or they were keeping some wild animals in there. When questioned what his dad was up to, Butch wouldn't say a word. But me and Ralphie, we were stellar detectives. One night we stayed up to spy on Butch's dad. We saw him and Butch unloading all kinds of boxes. Now that we knew that Butch's dad was just a thief and not some kind of axe murderer, it was a bit comforting. Maybe that's what made Butch's dad so mean?

Maybe it was the stress of finding stuff to steal and the possibility of getting caught that kept him on the edge? We were relieved and we were happy to keep Butch's and his dad's secret. After all, it was the code of the park. Nobody snitched. We all remained "as sick as our secrets."

The Big Bang

One day we were all playing near Ralphie's trailer when we heard gun fire. We all recognized that sound. In our trailer park, we were very familiar with the sound of guns being fired off occasionally. But this was different. This seemed purposeful, loud, and continuous. Somebody was hunting people. Tony told everyone to keep down and to stay flat on the ground.

Suddenly, there was a sound that none of us had ever heard before. It sounded and felt like a nuclear bomb had just been dropped on the park. Even after the initial shake of the blast, we all were still shaking with fear. We couldn't see much from where we were hiding but it sounded like it ripped metal apart. We stayed there, being as quiet as we could. Tony kept shushing our crying and whimpering so that whoever it was who did this horrible thing or whoever it was who was hunting people, could not find and kill us.

After we heard the cops and fire trucks arrive, we thought that we might be safe. So, we ventured out to see what had happened. The cloud of smoke and lights were in the direction of my area of the park. We moved closer. We peered out from around a trailer that was close enough for us to see what was happening without anyone seeing us. It was then that we saw everything. We just stood there, in silence. We saw the charred, crumpled and bullet-riddled remains of my home. There was very little left of my family's trailer. The roof had blown completely off, and bullet holes riddled my home from the back to the front. The walls themselves were opened up and spread outward like a flower in bloom. The firemen had not been able to put out all of the flames. We could still see fire and smoke billowing from my home. No one had to tell me, somehow, I just knew, that my parents could not have survived what I was seeing. The meth lab had exploded from the gunfire striking the chemicals that were stored inside of the trailer. My dad thought the chemicals were way too valuable to store in a shed outside. So, we lived and slept practically right on top of them.

    I knew that the motorcycle gang, "Demon Venom," had warned my dad to stop independently making meth. They had even offered my dad to come work for them. My dad was a way better meth cook than their sloppy cooks. With our superior product, many of their customers were coming to us. Dad had to know that that would anger the D.V. gang but dad only saw the money he was making. Money and meth were his gods, and that had proved fatal for he and mom. I could have been in there too, if not for play time. Now, my mom, my dad, my home, the money, and the meth had all gone up in the explosion. The notorious Demon Venom gang had sent their Annihilators, a special kill squad, to kill my whole family including me.

    Ruthie held me as I cried uncontrollably. I cried for my parents, but, also, I cried because I was scared. I didn't know what would happen to me, now. I couldn't show my face in public. I figured that I was a dead kid walking. It could be just a matter of time before I met the same fate as my parents. Dad and mom had made me be a part of their criminal activities, especially with the sales, pickups, and deliveries. I never wanted to do all of that stuff. I just wanted to be a kid. Now, I felt like I knew too much. I knew all of that information. I even knew my father's formula for making his product. I knew too much for the gang to let me live. I feared people would recognize me and point me out. Maybe a bounty was on my head! All I knew was that I had better hide.

    So, I hid in the one place that I knew nobody could find me. I hid in Ralphie's 'Where's Waldo' hiding place. The hideout my friend Ralphie used when he wanted to be invisible. It was under the trailer of the notorious "Green Lady". She had the fictitious reputation of eating kids. All of us kids would spread the rumor that she ate kids from near and far. The fact that she was grouchy, fed into the rumor until it went viral. No one went near her trailer. There was a loose piece in the lattice that closed off her crawlspace. It gave Ralphie access to create a comfy little hiding place right under her trailer. He had a couple of blankets laid out like carpet and pillows he had stolen from patio furniture. Like Ralphie, I had to be brave and quiet to stay there so long. Who knows what

CHARLES LEE KNUCKLES

would happen if the Green Lady discovered a kid right under her lair.

I peered from the hiding place and I watched all of the investigative activity. Detectives were going from door to door. They covered the whole trailer park, they even came to the Green Lady's front door, but they never saw me.

I figured that no one could find me. That is, until Ralphie scooted right in and said, "I knew you would be here, Little Tommy."

"Yeah, Ralphie, your hiding place is the best hiding place in the whole world. Tell me, what's going on out there? Is the coast clear yet?"

"Look Tommy, I don't know a better way to say it, but they recovered your parents' bodies. I guess they took them to the morgue and they hauled away your trailer. The detectives are still trying to find out why all of this happened. They are looking all over for you, Tommy."

He just sat there while I whimpered and cried.

I slept under that trailer that night. The next day, since we were about the same size, Ralphie brought me some clean clothes and he took mine to wash. To my name, I only had the clothes on my back and whatever was in my pockets. I dared not to come out of my hiding place, but on cold nights, Ralphie would sneak me into his house to sleep on his bedroom floor.

One night while I was looking at the starry sky through Ralphie's bedroom window, he asked me, "How long are you going to do this? Dude, you're starting to look like a wild kid, and you don't smell so good."

ADOPTED

"Ralphie, I don't want to live like this but if the cops catch me, there's no telling where they are going to send me. And if the Demon Venom catch me, they are going to kill me for sure."

We both sighed.

Then Ralphie said, "You've got a point dude." We drifted off to sleep.

Back to School

Even Butch, the bully, was kind to me, "Here little dude, I know you've got to be hungry. Take this food. It was free. I just took it off a kid at school."

For a kid of few words and even fewer kind words, this was the good side of Butch, the trailer park family side. I guess now that was my only family. Usually, I wouldn't approve of taking another kid's food. But this time, because I was starving, I scarfed it right down.

The sisters, Charlie and Ruthie, continued to bring me a little food and sit with me to talk. It was Charlie who suggested, "Turn yourself in Tommy. Just walk up to a cop and tell him who you are and what happened. They will find a better place for you to live."

"Yeah, but suppose they don't? Suppose they put me in Juvie with a bunch of criminals?"

"Tommy, they won't do that, will they? After all, it's not like you've committed a crime."

ADOPTED

"Charlie, I don't think I want to take that chance. I just want to stay here, where it's safe."

Charlie looked me in the eyes and said, "It's not all that safe here Tommy. It's never been safe."

I don't know how I stayed sane. Sometimes I wonder if I am sane. If not for my friends who treated me like family, I would have had a meltdown. But how long could this last? I know I couldn't grow up living under the Green Lady's trailer.

I don't know why I did it, but one day, I walked into school and sat down at my old desk. My hair was long and unkept. I must have looked like a feral cat. As the old folks might say, I smelled a bit musty. My clothes were dirty. Even though all the kids started to murmur at the sight of me, the teacher, Mrs. Monahan, acted as if everything was normal. She made no change in her schedule, like a regular day she did roll-call. She even called out my name, even though I'm pretty sure that my name was struck off the list by that time. Then, in keeping like this was just a normal day, she gave us a class assignment. I had nothing with me so she gave me a pencil and paper so that I too could do the assignment.

As we worked, Mrs. Monahan quietly stepped out of the room. She had been gone for only a few minutes, then she returned and resumed our lesson. She was as cool and calm as could be, she acted like it was normal for me to be there stinking up the place. I guess she was trying to keep me from panicking.

It was close to the end of the class when a CPS worker quietly walked into the room. Ms. Monahan, calmly, asked me to go with the worker.

The CPS guy looked at me, and he said, "Hi Tommy, I'm Mr. Thomas and people have been worried about you. We've been looking all over for you. You don't need to worry; you are not in trouble. We just want to make sure that you are well cared for and safe. Now let's get you ready for your new home. You're going to love it."

With my survival skills, I am able to size people up pretty quickly. I sized Mr. Thomas up in a few covert glances. I kind-of thought that I could outrun him, but I wasn't sure.

Mr. Thomas led me to his car. It was a jeep truck, the kind that I've always wanted. It had big tires and if you wanted to ride in style, you could take off the roof. I wanted to ride in this thing, but as we drove off, I had the overwhelming urge to jump out of the jeep and run as fast as I could back to my hiding place at the trailer park. It took everything in me to calm down. Mr. Thomas noticed my uneasiness and he gave me a smile. I was literally shaking at first, but the calm way Mr. Thomas spoke to me and that reassuring smile of his, helped me to relax.

Mr. Thomas glanced over at me as we sped down the road and said, "Tommy, you are a very fortunate boy to be able to get into the place where I'm taking you. It's in a great location and the owner really cares about kids. Just wait until you see this place. It's got horses, boats and a bunch of kids you're going to like."

The way Mr. Thomas talked about this place made me want to see it all the more. Before I knew it, I no longer felt like I wanted to jump out of the car. Besides, by this time I didn't even know where we were. We clearly were not in the

ADOPTED

city anymore. As I looked around there were big farms and ranches, like nothing I had ever seen before. It seemed like they were spaced really far apart. I had no clue as to where Mr. Thomas was taking me. Watching the long road whiz pass the car window made me relax a little deeper. I hadn't slept very well on the run. I tried to stay awake but I was exhausted. I must have nodded off.

For the first time in a long while, as I slept, my dreams weren't filled with the horrible nightmares of my home blowing up. I had also had nightmares of me being hunted by the Demon Venom gang. But now I was dreaming that Mr. Thomas had let me drive his jeep through the woods and on the beach. I was giving it full throttle when I was gently awakened.

I heard Mr. Thomas' voice saying, "Tommy, Tommy, wake-up, son. We're here."

I opened my eyes and looked up just in time to see the sign 'The Wright Farm' flow by overhead. Waking out of my sleep, I asked, "What is this place? Am I to be a farmer now?"

Then Mr. Thomas smiled and said, "This, my friend, is an orphanage for boys. It's a great place to be, Tommy. You, my friend, are a very lucky boy, that there's an opening here just for you! This place has got everything you need to grow up a successful young man."

As I looked around, I saw boys of all ages walking around with books and backpacks. There were adults with "Wright Farm" printed on the left front of their yellow t-shirts and in big print on the back, the word, "STAFF". This seemed to be a busy place. The atmosphere here was nothing like the trailer camp. I didn't know why, but I suddenly remembered the conversation with Charlie about it not being safe in the trailer park. But now, for the first time in a very long time, I felt safe.

A tall man came over and introduced himself to me. "Hi, you must be Tommy, I'm Will Jamison. I'll show you where you're going to be living. Grab your stuff and you can drop it off in your cabin. You've got a big day ahead of you, Tommy O'Connor. Welcome to the Wright Farm."

Rashawn

My name is Rashawn Wright. I wasn't always a member of the Wright family. I was born as Rashawn Richardson in abject poverty to Shirley Richardson. I never knew my father. I think his name was Jimmy Woods, but there's no real proof of who, actually, was my father. I was adopted by the Wright family. Now I have a mom, a dad, a sister, and two brothers. My family is awesome!

Currently, I am an attorney for my father's law firm in New York. People tell me that I am pretty good at what I do. I owe it all, everything, to my dad, David Wright. What a big surprise--who knew that I would grow up to be a corporate lawyer working in a prestigious law firm in Manhattan? The answer is, Nobody! Who knew that I would give my life to Christ and become a Christian? Once again, that answer would be a big, fat Nobody!

Religion did not seem to be relevant in the old neighborhood where I was born. Looking back, there seemed to be very little good in my old neighborhood. It felt like there was an assault on my soul. A coordinated attempt to darken my worldview. Although I knew nothing about spiritual things, back then, there seemed to be a spiritual battle to turn what little hope I had into hate. Fortunately for me all of that changed, first, when I met, my new brother, Tommy O'Connor. Then, everything really changed when I was adopted by my new dad, David Wright, and my new mother, Susan Wright.

My brother, Tommy, and I were so different. He is short, and I am tall. He is white and I am black. We had many other differences, but what we had in common outweighed them all. Hope and love had won out over our hate and dismay. I loved my brother Tommy from the moment we first spoke.

The reason I became a lawyer like my dad is simple. It was because I wanted to be just like my new dad. Dad was and is, even to this day, hands down, the best, healthiest, male role model that I had ever met. Ever since I've known dad, I've watched him in how he helps people. When dad came into my life, that's when I rediscovered that I had that same desire to love to help people, I just didn't know the best ways to help people. Dad really helped me to know altruism. Helping people was rare where I was born and raised. You didn't see examples of altruism often; everybody had ulterior motives, if they ever did anything for you. Even still, I've always managed to find hope, and a reason to be kind. Although I was extremely street savvy, I still looked for the good in people.

As a kid, I lived in one of the most poverty-stricken cities in Virginia. From what I've heard, it became so poor and run down after all the industry left the area.

ADOPTED

It seems that the industry jobs were replaced by welfare and crime. Neither welfare nor crime offered much hope. In fact, each fed off of the other.

Our neighborhoods were so dangerous that they devoured what good that was left of the traditional family. Fatherless families became the norm. Whole blocks of homes were run down and many houses were abandoned and taken over by gangs. Some of the single mothers turned to prostitution. Many people joined gangs and sold drugs. People, in general, did anything that was available so they could survive. Many fathers turned to crime or any hustle that was permitted by the gangs. The whole concept of family was changed. Now, for many kids, the gangs were their family.

Addiction, rape, robberies, and murder were so common that it was normal. People walked right past crimes in progress. There were two types of people in my neighborhood--victims and predators. No one escaped. We called the neighborhood, "The Trap." The Trap, one way or another, touched every family. One had to learn how to survive in this hostile and dangerous place.

The people who lived outside of this strange bubble didn't think much about the struggle that goes on with the people who lived in the bubble. It was like another world that they only saw on the nightly news. People really can't imagine living with this level of stress daily. Normally, people would no more think of visiting The Trap any more than you would think of visiting Mars.

I didn't have a gang name. Everybody called me by my name, Rashawn. Sometimes, I almost wished that I had a gang name when I heard my name in a southern drawl. I lived right in the middle of that bubble. All of my life I had been surrounded by ruthless gangs. Yet, I was, as long as I can remember, painfully aware that I was different. Also, I was painfully aware that, unfortunately, the gangs hated and destroyed "different". Unless we who were 'different' were extremely lucky, any talented or gifted individual had little hope of developing their gifts or talents. We were targets. Knowing this fact of life, I hid my talents, I hid my different, but I refused to let my different die.

In my neighborhood, it is futile and often fatal to resist the norm of conforming to gang activity. Fortunately for me, I was strong, fast, smart, and most of all, I was determined not to be in a gang. Unfortunately, none of these attributes mattered much in a city filled with guns and young people eager to commit gun violence. I went through life knowing that, for me, it was just a matter of time before some other kid would end my life. It was impossible to get comfortable with the fact that kids in my old neighborhood had short life expectancies. My demise seemed imminent. However, I nurtured my hidden dreams, dreams that daily battled with the reality that I did not expect to grow old. Not in this neighborhood. There were very few older people. If there were older people, they didn't come out in public.

Two more things worked in my favor, other than being fast, strong and smart. One was that I still had a few allies in the neighborhood. Some of them were in the "4th Ave. Stone Killers." A couple of the guys I grew up with didn't hate me for not being a gang member. In the neighborhood in which I was born, raised, and did my limited traveling, the Stone Killers ran everything. They knew me and even though I did not officially join their gang, they tolerated me breathing their air. The other thing that saved me was an 'OG' or 'Original Gangster' named Bo-Clyde. Bo-Clyde's reputation struck fear in every gang member in the city. He was seriously connected. He was also known for, not only being an 'Annihilator,' but also being the most ruthless and methodical killer ever to operate on the entire east coast. Annihilators were called that because they not only would kill their target, but they also killed anyone that was closely associated with their target. They killed whole families.

    I worked for Bo-Clyde. He put me in the front of his store. Part of my duties was to restock the store shelves. Also, I was the person that rang up the legitimate purchases. Mr. Clyde trusted me to operate the cash register. However, I had no connection to his criminal activities. Even though I was underaged and could only work limited hours, I think that Mr. Clyde thought that my presence made him look legit. As I look back, I think that our relationship wasn't that complicated. I was looking for a masculine role model, a father figure. At the same time, Bo-Clyde's nasty career included killing people, so it forced him to think that having a family was a weakness that he could not afford. Now that Mr. Clyde was established, perhaps he was looking for a son. I think that in his mind I was his closest substitute for family, for a son. Even though I knew that, ultimately, I was expendable. Nevertheless, I was looking for a dad and he was older and for our neighborhood, established. I think that he was looking for a surrogate son--a son that was smart and could represent the good that he could never be associated with because of his past. I think he wanted to take some form of credit for who I was, in the sense that I was not evil. Maybe he wanted to be responsible for something good in the world before he grew old and died--the one good thing that he did in life. Well, maybe our relationship was a little complicated.

Unfortunately, to complicate matters even further, my mother, Shirley Richardson, was a heroin addict. Often, on the many nights that she was high on heroin, in between nods, she liked to read to me from the Bible. When she nodded off, I would read the Bible back to her. I don't know if I got much out of it at the time other than just the comfort of being with my mom. A lot of the time I would see her desperate for her next fix. She would act like someone possessed. I know now that deep down inside she was just desperate for a new life. She didn't want to be an addict; she just couldn't stop. There was nothing or no one to save her. Try as I might, I couldn't save her. It means a lot to me to remember the times we spent together reading the Bible. Not so much the Bible reading, but the peace it seemed to give us.

On the other hand, my father, or the 'sperm donor' as I called him, was a total mystery. He never had time for me. It was thought that my father was a man named Jimmy Woods, also known as Twist. The rumor was that he had disappeared because he had been killed by the Henderson Projects' Black Mafia Crew (BMC). His body was never found, so, who knows? I gave up trying to figure it out. My mom was dealing with so many men. Who knows for sure which one was my daddy? Anyway, nobody was stepping up to the plate. So, for the four to five hours while I was at work, I chose Bo-Clyde to be my father figure. In the same sense, he chose or hired me to be his son.

Still, at ripe old age of fourteen years young, my reality felt like I was on my own. The Housing Authority just barely kept that ratty old roof over my and mom's heads. It was just the two of us. Because the welfare benefits (money and food stamps) came in mom's name, they went directly to her dealers towards her addiction. At a very early age, I had to earn enough money to feed both mom and me. For my health and well-being, I had to do everything an adult should have been doing for me. I had to wash clothes, wash dishes and keep the house clean. I even had to dispose of my mom's drug paraphernalia.

I could have easily been swallowed up by the 'Stone Killers' to work selling drugs for them. A couple of times my mom even suggested that I sell dope. I think it was because she wanted access to more drugs and she was willing to use me to get them. I think she would have ripped me off in a heartbeat and left me to face the consequences. I didn't blame mom. I just couldn't blame her; she was sick. I saw the damage that addictions did to the whole neighborhood. Mom sometimes blamed her behavior on Eve eating the fruit from the forbidden tree in the Garden of Eden.

She would be high and say to me, "Oh my beautiful boy, don't ever eat of the fruit of the forbidden tree because it only brings death."

Whether she could hear me through her intoxication or not, I would just reply, "I know mom. I know."

ADOPTED

Rescued by a sympathetic old gangster

I worked for the gangster named Bo-Clyde. Mr. Clyde owned the neighborhood corner-store. That's where he would sell high-priced foods and other essentials just to cover for his other activities. The store looked legit but Bo-Clyde was also a loan shark. He made a dollar on each dollar from his money loans. In other words, if you borrowed $100, you had to quickly, without hesitation, pay Bo-Clyde back $200.00. These were not long-term loans. The turnover was fast. His other hustle was selling drugs. Not by the bag--he was a wholesaler. Because he was never in the same building with the stuff, no one could ever prove that he was involved. Bo-Clyde was into some high-level organized crime stuff. He financed criminal activities. I acted like I paid no attention to his illegal activities. I think he liked that I minded my own business, and I purposely knew nothing that would incriminate him. I also think that he intentionally insulated me from the dangers of his business.

Even with all the money floating through that store, nobody would dare rob Bo-Clyde's store. He had the only store in the neighborhood that didn't have to pay the Stone Killers' protection tax. He was protected at a much higher level. He was connected in a big way. Bo-Clyde was my safety net. I was very fortunate that Bo-Clyde had always demonstrated a fatherly nature when it came to me. I could feel it. Although he would occasionally issue stern orders to me, I always felt that they were out of concern for me.

To the local thugs, I was another piece of Bo-Clyde's property, and nobody touched Bo-Clyde's property and lived. It was odd that a killer would keep me from being killed. I look back now, and wonder, "Was God at work here? Did God use a bad man like Bo-Clyde to help a kid like me?"

Even with Bo-Clyde's protection, still there was danger around every corner in every alley throughout the area where I lived in the city. On my way to the store or on my way home, I had to travel through some very sketchy areas. Although I was considered Bo-Clyde's property, still I was not Bo-Clyde.

Bo-Clyde occasionally would have heart-to-heart talks with me. Bo would say to me, "Look kid I can't protect you everywhere. You're special, you still have morals," he would giggle. "I notice things. It's not out of fear that you are trustworthy. There are things that you just won't do. You are a light in the middle of darkness. I won't try to change that about you. So, I won't ever make you do things against your personal code.

ADOPTED

The problem for you is that, living in this part of the city, all those things that are against your code and that you don't want to do, eventually you're going to have to do them. Eventually, you've got to learn to enjoy doing the evil that you don't want to do in order to survive and keep your sanity. Why do you think these thugs don't rob me? Or when I loan even the most dishonest person money, they always pay me back?"

"I don't know Mr. Clyde. Maybe because you are so respected that even the toughest guys respect you?"

"No kid, there's no such thing as respect in this neighborhood. It's fear--they all fear me. It's funny that although I'm proud of it in front of other gangsters, I'm not proud of it in front of you. But at the same time, I enjoy the fact that the right people know that I enjoy hurting people and I'm highly skilled at it. I'm a killer. I kill for a living. I can run my business here because of my reputation of being dangerous."

I was looking down when Mr. Clyde was talking all that killing stuff. When he had finished, I looked up at him and said, "Yeah, but Mr. Clyde, I don't want people to fear me. I want to like people. I want friends."

Bo-Clyde took me by the chin to make me look him in the eyes, and said, "Don't be a sucker kid, you can't find friends around here."

Through teary eyes, without missing a beat and because I meant it, I said, "But I consider you as my friend Mr. Clyde."

At this, Bo Clyde was at a loss for words. He turned away quickly so I wouldn't see his face. Then, he just went back to the cash register and sat on his stool, facing away from me, pretending to count cash that he had already counted. I think that even though he thought attachments were weak spots, these kinds of moments made the gangster care for me even more.

Nobody knew where I got the hope that made me so positive in such a negative environment. I never knew why I was this way. This neighborhood was all I knew, and it was all out of hope. So where did my hope come from?

When my drug addict mother was sober enough, she would read the Bible to me. Despite all that I saw around me, I would try believe it. I believed in Christ Jesus and I never gave up hoping that a better world would come with His return. But I had no idea what that would even look like. I also wondered, did His love for the world include my neighborhood? Still, it was the only explanation I could figure for the hope that sustained me in such a hopeless place. Today, I thank God for that raggedy old Bible that I had found in the trash and that sat next to the needle and spoon in the corner on our old card table.

I saved all the money Bo-Clyde paid me. I kept it under a floorboard in my room. It was the perfect hiding place. I knew I had to hide my money from mom and any of her friends. It was always my dream that one day I would use that money to get mom and me out of this nasty old place. Sometimes, when I sat by myself, I would dream of the day that my mom would get sober and we would live in a nice home in a better neighborhood.

I used to say to her, "Mom, one day I'm gonna get us out of this rickety old house and out of this nasty neighborhood."

In her more lucid moments, she would say, "I know you will, son. I can't wait to get to our promise land." She would ask questions like, "Will there be a nice front porch on our new house? Will we sit on our front porch in our rocking chairs, and look out over our pretty front lawn, son?"

In our minds, we would go into what seemed like a different dimension of space and time. We would escape outside of our reality to an imaginary place of rest for our souls. A place with peace and tranquility. Instead of that dank and dark kitchen, we sat on our imaginary, bright, and airy front porch. We would talk about what flowers and vegetables we would plant in our gardens in the backyard. I just loved to see the smile that these times would put on mom's face.

Acts 2:17b, *"and your young men shall see visions, and your old men shall dream dreams."*

CHARLES LEE KNUCKLES

Daydreams turn into Nightmares

One day, when I was coming home from work, just as I entered the house, I heard some groaning and crying in the kitchen. Immediately, I rushed back to see if my mom was alright. What I saw next I will never forget. Some gang members were in my kitchen and one had my mom's hand over the hot stove. He was yelling, "Where's our dope old lady?"

As smoke filled the kitchen, I could smell her flesh burning. I tried to get to her but I was held back by two of the gang members. Mom's eyes were almost completely swollen shut from being punched. Her face was such a bloody mess I could hardly recognize her. There were four big guys, maybe in their early twenties, maybe younger. At 14 years old, they were much stronger than me. Two held me, the other two continued to loom over my mom. I was helpless as they laughed. "Now she'll talk! Hey Shirley, do you want to see your son die?"

ADOPTED

I was reminded of what Bo-Clyde said about enjoying hurting people. I could see that these monsters deeply enjoyed the evil that they were doing.

Through the blood streaming down her face, I could see mom's eyes look over at me. She screamed, "Run boy, run!"

I yelled at the thug in charge, "How much money does she owe you? I'll give it to you."

The lead guy got inches from my face and shouted like a madman, "Where is it, punk? You've got our money?"

"No sir, I don't have your money but I have money."

I took them back to my room, and I pulled up the floorboard where I hid my money. I held it in my hand one last time before it was snatched away. I said, "There's over five hundred dollars. It's all I've got."

The gang leader looked at me and smiled, I tried to be cool as I said, "This ain't your money. It's my money. I've saved it from my job. Now that you've got it, let her go."

All of his gold teeth shined as he grinned at me, "Where did you get all this money, ya lil' punk? You dealing in our territory or something?"

"No sir, I don't sell drugs. I work for Bo Clyde. He's not going to like it if you hurt us."

"We're not going to hurt you little man, but we're gonna to take your money, and your mom too."

Reality dug in and I started to cry, "But I paid you, now you can let her go!"

"Kid, this is not nearly enough. Besides, she stole from us. That kind of violation against the Stone Killers never goes unpunished."

As they dragged my mom out the door, I ran behind them grabbing for her until one thug turned and hit me so hard that he knocked me out cold. That was my last memory of the nightmare event. That was the last time that I would see my mom.

A normal person would have called the police and asked for help. This was not a normal neighborhood. Calling the police was an instant death sentence. Besides, the police did very little to help people in this neighborhood. And Bo-Clyde had warned me many times that if I ever called the cops, he would be finished with me. Without his protection I wouldn't last a day around here, and there would be no hope of getting my mom back.

I cried all night. I prayed and prayed as hard as I could. I yelled at God, "Aren't You going to do something?" I could find no rest, no sleep--where was my precious hope now? God was silent. He was not answering this kid's prayer. I thought to myself, "It's this neighborhood. God just doesn't come here."

The morning was chilly. I washed and got dressed. I didn't know what to do. So, I walked to work and I told Bo Clyde everything. I thought that he was my only friend.

Bo-Clyde looked at me and said, "Look kid your mom broke the code. There ain't nothing I can do about what happens next; it's the code of the streets."

I asked, "What's gonna happen next Mr. Clyde?"

"Kid, the hard fact is that you ain't never gonna see your mom again."

ADOPTED

He paused, as I cried so loud that I thought my body would collapse. I thought that I would die right there on the spot. The hurt, grief, and sadness were overwhelming. I have never felt anything like this in my life. I needed a shoulder to cry on, but Bo-Clyde would never permit me to cry on his shoulder.

He simply said, "As much as I like you kid, I can't be around you no more. You'll draw too much heat on my operation."

Deep down inside I knew that well enough to just accept it. As much as he and I fantasized, Bo-Clyde was not my father. Nor was he the father-figure that my survival instincts had created.

Mr. Clyde continued, "Is there anything that you want from your house? If there is anything, then go pack it up and come back."

I walked home slowly to an empty house. I was no longer concerned for my safety. I sat in my room, and I cried for what seemed like a long time. Then, I looked around the house one last time. After I gathered everything that I could fit into my duffle bag, like a robot with no emotions left in me, I headed back to Bo-Clyde's store. Mr. Clyde closed the store. Then, he took me to his car, and off we drove. The drive was silent until we arrived at the Child Protective Services building.

Mr. Clyde gave me a couple hundred dollars and said, "Hide this money and don't let nobody know that you have it. This is it for you. It's the last thing that you will ever get from me! Don't ever mention me to nobody! Do not even say my name again. You got that?"

"Yes sir Mr. Clyde. I get it." I had always known that in this world, I was on my own.

Mr. Clyde told me, "Go into that building and tell them that you've just lost your mom and you have nowhere to go. This is the last advice I'm going to give you. Sure, you are on your own, but you've got what it takes, kid. You are going to have a better life. Look, son." Every time Mr. Clyde called me 'son,' my ears would perk up. This time was no different. I enjoyed one last hope of sonship before he said, "You're going to be somebody special. Good luck kid. Now git!"

"There I stood, with my duffle bag in hand, as the CPS worker looked across her desk at me. "Son, what can I help you with today?"

My head hung down as I answered, "My mom is gone. I have no one now, and a friend whose name I cannot mention told me to come here. Can you help me?"

The kindly desk receptionist sounded like a mom as she asked in the gentlest voice, "Kid, what happened to your mother?"

"I don't know. She was carried off by some mean men. I think she's probably dead by now."

As I started to cry, the kind lady came from around her desk and hugged me. The emotions I thought had gone, came flooding back. The pain I felt was overwhelming. Once again, I thought that I was going to die right then and there, on the spot, from sadness. In her arms, I let it all go. My body became limp. The kind lady held me up and I cried big, heaving sobs and moans from my gut. I thought my life was over. How could I go on living through this pain? The lady just let me cry myself out. Then, she walked me into a room and gave me a sandwich and an orange soda. I didn't have an appetite but she convinced me to eat.

From there, a CPS worker took me to what they called a group home, but it looked more like a prison. As we walked through the gates into the first building, I saw a bunch of boys from different neighborhoods. There were boys from all the different gangs of the city. I knew that I was in danger because I didn't belong to a gang. I could lose everything--my money, the nice clothes Mr. Bo-Clyde gave me, and I could even lose my life.

As soon as we were alone, a big kid walked up to me. "What's up? Who you with?"

I recognized him from the 4th Avenue area. He had to be a member of the Stone Killers gang.

I got right in his face and shouted, "None of your business."

Before he could swing, I punched him in the mouth. He tried to punch me back but I didn't allow him to hit me, I smothered him with a combination of punches. I kept him in front of me, so that I couldn't be ambushed from behind, I kept my back close to the wall. In order to avoid being everybody's target and to keep my stuff from being stolen, I had to win this fight. I had to win it violently and decisively. With no weapon, he had to fight me hand-to-hand and he was not up to the task of a fair fight. I won that fight easily. Now, the fact that I was not to be messed with was well established. But would that be enough?

CHARLES LEE KNUCKLES

The Truth hurts

The day room where everyone milled around and watched TV was huge. Naturally, the room was divided up by which gang the guys were in. Each gang had their areas. Because the staff used my address to assign me an area, I was assigned to a bunk in the Stone Killers section. I finished stowing all of my gear under my bunk. As I turned around, a Stone Killer gang member even bigger than the one I had just defeated was right in my face. I knew, just like his buddy, I would have to take him down quickly.

Before I could take my first swing, the gang member blurted out something that instantly buckled my knees, "You don't even know that it was Bo-Clyde who killed your mom."

I was struck to the core. I screamed, "You're a liar, you're a stinking liar!"

He stepped back so I couldn't hit him and said calmly, "You can call me what you want, Rashawn. See, I even know your name, punk. Still, that doesn't change the facts; nothing will. Bo-Clyde had to kill your mom. She was just another junkie! And she had the nerve to steal her dealer's stash. Ha! It was Bo-Clyde's stash. How stupid are you? You've got to know that he controls everything in the hood."

Hearing all the commotion, especially my gut-wrenching screams of, "You're a dirty, stinking lair," the staff came running into the room. By the time they got to us, I had collapsed at the kid's feet. He and other members of the Stone Killers had just started stomping and kicking me. I didn't fight back this time. I couldn't even bother to defend myself. I was a blubbering mess. Everybody knew about my mom and the man I looked up to as a father figure. I thought that I had seen a lot of dirty stuff, but this was way too much to bear. I had finally been broken. Early in life, I learned that you never show weakness in front of gang members. But now, there I was, on the floor in the fetal position, collapsed and crying out loud like a baby.

The one friend I thought I had turned out to be a monster in disguise. The monster that had killed my mom. All of this time, I had protected the only hope that I had, but now, I was drained of all hope. There was no light to be salvaged. How could there be a God? What had I done for Him to hate me so much? How could He let this happen? If God was anything like my deadbeat dad or Bo-Clyde, from then on, I wanted nothing to do with Him.

That was when I first met Mr. Thomas. He was an ex-marine and a giant of a man. I was on the ground, curled up in a ball. I was a quivering mess, and I was crying my eyes out. No punch had put me down. Words had floored me. Just as the kids were starting to kick me, Mr. Thomas, hearing the commotion, led the staff charging into the room. He took one look at the situation, then he yelled "Stop!" His voice was so powerful and had so much authority that everything just stopped. For a second, it even felt like time stopped.

I was down on the floor. I was surrounded by a gang of kids that had been stomping and kicking me. Mr. Thomas ran through the crowd and stood over me like a great protector. Then, he lifted me up off the floor with his massive hands like I was light as a feather. Strangely enough, as firm as he was to the gang members, he was equally gentle to me, as he said calmly, "Get your stuff, kid, and follow me."

I didn't realize it then, but I know now, that God was giving me, through Mr. Thomas, a glimpse of the image of Christ, reassuring me that He was still with me. But my hope and faith were still gone. Restoration wasn't going to come so easily. I still felt abandoned and betrayed.

I didn't know it at the time, and I imagine that Bo-Clyde didn't realize it, but what helped me were his orders, "Whatever you do, don't kill the boy, and do not kill his mom in front of him." As Bo-Clyde had said many times, he lived by the code of the streets. No one steals from the organization and lives. But I'd like to think that Bo-Clyde was sad about what he had done. I knew that he lived a life in which he could never show weakness, because if he did, his time in leadership would be over. He would be over.

Mr. Thomas took me into an office. The man looked at me for a moment, and then he asked bluntly, "What gang are you with?"

"I ain't with no gang," I replied.

ADOPTED

Mr. Thomas then looked at me even deeper into my eyes, and said slowly, "I'm not in a gang, sir, is the proper response, son."

I hung my head ashamedly, and said, "I know sir, but you can't talk all proper in my neighborhood and survive."

"It didn't look like you were surviving out there a few minutes ago. Just how did you survive not being a gang member?"

"Barely, sir, just barely."

I had been warned. From my street-smarts and out of pure fear, I didn't even want to speak the name "Bo-Clyde." So even though that was the right answer, I wasn't going to say that the same man that had killed my mom was also my source of survival. I was still confused about how could Bo-Clyde treat me so well, and yet, so cold-bloodedly kill my mother?

Mr. Thomas interrupted my thoughts, "You're not going back into that room. It would be bad for you if I sent you back in there. Probably a death sentence. I can't do that. Is this everything you have?"

"Yes, sir, it's all I have to my name." I didn't mention the money that I had stashed in my underwear.

"Wait here son, I've got to talk to the rest of the staff."

I waited, still thinking about how could I had been so wrong about Mr. Clyde? How could he do such a thing? Then, I started to think about revenge, but only for a minute and I quickly dismissed those thoughts. I knew that nobody like me could take Bo-Clyde out. Besides, even as empty as I was emotionally, I still was not cold-blooded enough to kill or even hurt anybody. Even if there was a rare chance that I could find an opportunity, there's no way that I could do anything like that. There was nothing I could do but cry. So, I just sat and cried.

I remembered reading something in the Bible with my mom about vengeance, and not repaying evil for evil, but I still wanted to do something. And even though I didn't know what I wanted to do, I desperately wanted to do something. My thoughts continued to wander. Anyway, if vengeance belonged to God, how come Bo-Clyde is still walking around, doing what he does? I decided right then and there that I would be mad at God, that maybe, I would have nothing to do with Him!

When Mr. Thomas returned, he flew through the door. There was a huge smile on his face and he could barely contain his excitement. The speed of how fast he was talking made things even more exciting. "Look kid, when I first saw you, you were fighting. But while talking to you, I saw a glimpse of hope." Suddenly he switched to a slower gear, and he asked me, "Where do you get your hope from, kid?"

Surprised, I paused for a second, "You saw hope in me, sir?"

"Yes, Rashawn, I saw hope in you. Is that so crazy?"

"I don't rightly know sir. I thought that I had lost all hope. And you're sure that you saw hope in me?"

"Grab your bag, kid, you're getting out of here. I'm going to take a chance on you, Rashawn! You'd better not let me down! We're going to the Wright Farm!"

ADOPTED

It seemed like all hope was gone, and then, because a man like no man I had ever met before, said that he saw some hope, I began to regain my strength, and a little spark of hope.

There we were, riding in Mr. Thomas's jeep. With the ease of a humming motor, we sailed down the country roads. The sun was shining and it was warm outside as we headed for the orphanage called the Wright Farm. Mr. Thomas had his jeep's windows down and the wind blew through the jeep. The country air smelled differently. I don't think that I knew that city air smelled so differently until I smelled country air. It was so fresh and clean--nothing at all like the polluted air in the city. The car stereo was playing some unfamiliar music, but the beat was tight.

So, I asked, "Mr. Thomas, what's that music?"

"That's Christian rap, Rashawn. Do you like it?"

I replied, "Hmmm, Christian rap? I didn't know there was such a thing. It is kinda tight. I think I do like it. But Mr. Thomas, right now, I'm against Christianity!"

"That's sad, son. I only listen to Christian music. There's Christian music in every genre. I listen to Christian rock, Christian Gospel music, Christian country music and, of course, Christian Rap." He smiled and said, "Want me to play some Christian Folk music? Cause I've got that too."

"Nah." I said, "I'm good with this."

On the drive, I seemed to forget about all of my problems as we got to talking about music.

Mr. Thomas said, "I never listen to secular music."

"What's secular music, Mr. Thomas?"

He thought for a second, "I think it's a term given to any music that is not Christian. Secular came from a Latin word that means 'the world'. That's why you will hear many Christians call it 'worldly music.' That's mainly because it concerns things of the world in general, and not things that are sacred. Rashawn, to me, Christian artists are much more talented because they don't take the easy route, like using cuss words to attract the ears of young people. There are no evil messages to incite violence or foolish behavior. Also, to me, all Christian music has a positive vibe and spiritually healthy message. By the way, you'll hear a lot of Christian music at the Farm. The Wright Farm is run by a Christian man"

"What is this Farm, sir? I don't think that I know how to be a farmer. What are the requirements to be on the Farm? Do I have to be a certain kind of Christian? Are there gangs there?"

"Rashawn, it might feel a little scary to you because you are going into an unknown environment. I know that you have questions and I will try to answer them all. Don't worry, son. This farm is like no place you've ever experienced before. There are no gangs, it's safe, and no, you don't have to be Christian to be accepted at the Farm. The educational program is exceptional. They can and will do everything possible to help you get into college."

I asked, "College? But Mr. Thomas, nobody from my neighborhood gets into college. Don't get me wrong, I do want to go to college! But I never dreamed I would have any kind of chance to be a college student!"

ADOPTED

Suddenly, this new information opened up for me a whole new dream world. Immediately, my list of the possibilities and my imagination soared to new heights.

Mr. Thomas brought me back down to earth, "Rashawn! Earth to Rashawn? Listen to me, if you work hard, you can do things that never would have happened for you in your old neighborhood. You can graduate from college. At the Wright Farm you can change the trajectory of your life. However, in the meantime you will have to do some farming chores, but all in all, it'll be fun. Rashawn, there's something else you may notice about the Farm. That is, at least from what I've been told, they say that God's presence is everywhere. And they also say that at the Farm, the goodness of God produces fellowship and good friendships. You will gain new friendships that have absolutely nothing to do with gangs. And even folks that don't know God, find God at the Farm. Rashawn, realistically, for some kids, the Farm will just be a farm. But for others, the Farm is an opportunity. A gift from God. Son, I hope that you can find a way to let your eyes see every opportunity."

"Mr. Thomas, I'm so mad at God, I don't know if I can ever forgive Him."

Mr. Thomas eased the car over to the side of the road. And then he turned to face me. He took a deep breath, then he smiled and looked me in the eyes. He asked me, "So can I ask, why are you so against God?"

I answered his question with a question that had been haunting me for a long time. "Well sir, I thought that I knew God, but He let my mom die. I just can't figure out why did your God have to let my momma become an addict and die such a horrible death?"

Mr. Thomas paused. I could see in his face that just like I felt it, he also felt my pain. The expression on Mr. Thomas' face made it clear to me that he was very familiar with the pain that I was feeling. It was then that I knew, even before he answered, that my question had hit Mr. Thomas hard. He was taking my question very seriously. That was very important to me. It made me know that whatever he was going to say would be something real. I had let myself be vulnerable in front of someone who cared. Perhaps now, he was going to agree with me and support my anger at God?

Then Mr. Thomas slowly came out of his pause, "Hmmm, let me see; how can I put this? Rashawn, first, I've got to tell you that I lost my brother to addiction. My brother Jimmy had a brilliant mind. We all admired Jimmy for his cleverness on just about any topic. Jimmy was smart and he had all the right advantages in life. We weren't poor. We had both our mom and our dad. We didn't live in a bad neighborhood. And yet, Jimmy became an addict and ultimately died from an overdose of heroin. I was so angry at everything. I was angry at Jimmy. I was angry at the dealers. I was angry about addiction, and yes, Rashawn, I, too, was angry at God. I literally wanted to hunt and kill the people who profited from selling drugs."

I wanted to interrupt Mr. Thomas and confess that I wanted to kill Bo-Clyde. But I didn't. I just listened as he continued. Mr. Thomas paused for a second and a couple of tears fell down his face.

ADOPTED

"Later, I had a friend during my time in the Marines that was like a brother to me. One day, when we were on patrol, while he was smiling at me about something silly I had said, right before my eyes a sniper shot him in the head. He died instantly. He fell into my arms and I carried him to the other side of the Humvee. I cradled his body in my arms and cried. Then, I laid him body down, took up my weapon and fired every round that was in its magazine in the direction of the sniper. I wanted to kill everybody in that area that wasn't American. I was so angry that, not fearing for my own safety, I charged the sniper's position, firing until I saw him slump over and fall from a rooftop. For a long time, I carried that anger and it turned me into a bitter person. Deep down inside, I knew that God had nothing to do with these tragedies. But I was still mad at Him. Later, looking back, I came to realize that God was right by my side through it all. I only had to turn to Him to make my pain into something better than bitterness.

"Rashawn, when I turned back to God, I found my calling in helping kids like you to not be consumed by evil. Evil deeds done to people often turns people into evil doers. Don't let your mom's killers recruit you into being an evil doer. Through it all, turn to your heavenly Father for strength and guidance. Get better, not bitter. God has nothing to do with evil, and addiction is evil. It was created by evil people from the inspiration of demonic forces. It appeals to man's lust for profit. Addiction is used to control people. As sad as we are about the impact of addiction, it also makes God sad. He is right there beside you, grieving for your mother with you. Don't block Him out when you need Him the most. Let something good come out of it all.

"Another thing, Rashawn. God has no desire to make us into His puppets, so He has given us the freedom to turn to Him or the freedom to reject Him. It's His gift to us, and it's called free will. People misinterpret and misuse both freedom and free will all the time. But God will not take His gifts back. It's people that take away other people's freedom and free will, not God. People enslave others for twisted, ungodly reasons. At the same time, without knowing it, they even enslave themselves to the evil one. God created this world and then He handed it over to us to have dominion, but we've created systems that govern with pain and destruction rather than with love. God gave us more than enough on this planet to share and to enjoy. But we hoard from one another and seek to control each other. Rashawn, I don't know how your mom fell into the trap of addiction, but I can assure you that it was not of God's doing. God had nothing to do with your mom's death. But I'm willing to bet that He's with her right now, comforting her and that now, she is finally free."

Mr. Thomas looked at the road, and said, "God didn't do any of that to you, me, my brother Jimmy, or your mom, Rashawn. He loves you and your mom. He was right there with her when she took her last breath. He is right here with you and I right now in your sadness and grief. He feels every bit as sad as you."

I looked at Mr. Thomas. Now, I had tears in my eyes too. I started to cry really hard. I knew that this was my opportunity to forgive myself for being so mean to God. But I still had one more question. I asked, "Mr. Thomas, why does God let evil people get away with so much evil?"

This time, he looked off into the distance while answering, "Rashawn, I suspect that it's not God that lets evil prosper, it's man. I don't think that we'll ever fully understand why we don't take responsibility for our evil. There's an evil of which many good people are guilty. That's the evil of doing nothing about evil. The evil of doing nothing about the evil that goes on in our world brings us unwittingly in concert with the evil we fear. I think what we have to do is to learn how to not tolerate evil and greed, so that we don't unwittingly become evil ourselves. We must learn how to forgive our enemies in a way that both holds them accountable and reveals the power of good. I think that we have to learn how to give stuff over to Christ and not let evil define our lives so that we can operate in good on a stronger level. Now, Rashawn, I guess the real question is, what are you going to do with your free will and freedom? You have the freedom to choose whose side you are going to be on. Will it be with God?"

"Dang, Mr. Thomas, when you put it like that..." For the first time in a long while I was smiling again. "Mr. Thomas, I guess I was mad at God over the stuff where I had no control. I figure that the only control I do have is to choose how I respond to what happened. Sir, I think that I'm on God's side, but what should I do now?"

"Rashawn, now you pray."

I asked Mr. Thomas to pray, but he said, "Rashawn, this is between you and God. Take a moment and send God a silent prayer, son."

CHARLES LEE KNUCKLES

We both did a moment of silent prayer.

Mr. Thomas was so good at getting my mind off negative thoughts, that I decided that one day I'd like to be just like Mr. Thomas. I silently asked God to forgive me for talking to Him so mean. After my silent prayer for forgiveness, it seemed like things got better. Maybe my attitude was getting better. Maybe it was then that I got a bit more of my hope back. After we prayed, Mr. Thomas got back on the road, and we rocked out on his Christian music.

The ride was so much fun that I decided that I really liked Mr. Thomas. We were friends. We played the license plate game. The first person to call an out-of-state license plate gets a point. Then, I also learned how to play "Punch Buggy, No Punch Backs." That's when you spot a Volkswagen Beetle and you lightly punch the other person in the shoulder and yell, "Punch Buggy, No Punch backs." I wonder what Mr. Thomas was thinking because he was punching me way lighter than I was punching him. By the way, I won that game, too. While it's true that I was doing all the winning, I'll probably never know if Mr. Thomas was just letting me win to bring me out of my funk. It seemed like we laughed the whole drive.

Then, I'll never forget when Mr. Thomas suddenly pointed and said, "Look. We're here." It seemed eerie how quiet it got in the jeep.

I looked up as we rode under a sign that simply read, "The Wright Farm." The driveway seemed very long, and regardless of Mr. Thomas' pep-talk, I was still a little scared. The wounded kid in me just wanted to ask, "Mr. Thomas, can I just stay with you?" But I didn't want to appear to be a frighten little

ADOPTED

kid, even though that's exactly what I was--a frightened kid. So, I clammed up.

Mr. Thomas seemed to sense my fears. "Don't worry Rashawn, this place is just what you need. It's perfect for you, and you're perfect for it. You're going to love it here. You're going to see and do things that you would have never had the chance to see and do where you lived before."

Mr. Thomas stopped in front of a building that said 'Office'. A tall man with a cowboy hat walked over and shook Mr. Thomas' hand. They acted like they were old friends as they laughed and exchanged greetings. Then, they turned and looked at me.

Mr. Thomas took my self-imposed drama out of the moment by saying to the man, "Mr. Will, I'd like you to meet Rashawn, the kid we spoke about earlier."

The first words that Mr. Will spoke to me were, "Hi, Rashawn, grab your gear and let's get it stowed away in your new dorm. Rashawn, you and Mr. Thomas are just in time for dinner. It's Shepard's Pie with green beans, corn, and the best collard greens you've ever tasted."

Mr. Thomas chimed in, "That sounds delicious. I could eat. What about you Rashawn?"

Still a bit intimidated by it all, I forced a smile and said, "Yeah, I'm hungry as a bear."

I was still nervous as heck. On this Farm, I was way out of my element. I remember asking myself, "Can I even do this?" And then, answering myself, "Of course you can. Don't be a scaredy-cat!"

Mr. Will showed me my cabin and my bunk. As I was stowing my gear, I noticed someone else was there. He spoke to me from the shadow of the lower bunk. As ominous as it was with the shadow and to not see him fully, he had a friendly enough voice.

"Hey dude, people call me, Little Tommy. I guess we're going to be bunkies now. I've got the bottom bunk. You're up top. The ladder is on the front. I try to keep my bunk sharp. So, when you're climbing up to your bunk, please don't step on mine."

Then Mr. Will asked him, "Hey, Tommy, can you show Rashawn how to get to the cafeteria when he's done getting settled?"

"Sure, Mr. Will, I've got him."

As Mr. Will was walking away, he yelled back, "You're going to be just fine, Rashawn. Relax."

I looked to see where the friendly voice had coming from. It was then that Little Tommy stood up from out of the shadow. There he was, Little Tommy. He was a short, slightly-built, white guy. He had blue eyes and blond hair with a flattop haircut. And he had this big old smile. I was fresh out of the city, with its gangs and set boundaries. I didn't know what to think.

Naively, I asked, "Hey, man, are we even supposed to be in the same bunk house? I mean you're white and I'm black?"

With that big old smile, Lil Tommy said, "Duuude! I thought the same thing when I first got here." Tommy got closer and lowered his voice, "Dude, When I first got here, I figured that

ADOPTED

it was going to be like juvie. You know how they separated us by gangs and color?"

Then, he stood up straighter and pursed his lips, blowing through them making a fluttering sound. When he had finished making that sound, he said, "But Mr. Will don't play that stuff here. In every way, he shows us that we can all live together. We can all be friends and even be brothers. Oh, yeah! Wait until you see his lady, dude! She's so beautiful and she ain't white."

It was hard for me to take it all in, because of the way things were in every poor neighborhood where I had lived. So, I said, "Yeah, but where I come from everybody's from gangs and the white gangs live on the other side of town. Let me see your tattoos."

"I ain't got none, dude. Let me see yours."

"I ain't got none, either. I don't run with a crew."

Tommy replied, "I don't run with any gang either."

It was like somebody had turned on a light bulb in my brain. I said, hesitantly, "Maybe here, Tommy, in this place, we can just be friends."

I smiled at my new friend. I thought that everybody called him Little Tommy because of his size. So, I decided that I wasn't going to do the same. I'm going to do just the opposite. "Yeah, maybe here you can be my big bro'?" We both laughed.

Tommy, smiling, said, "Me, your big bro'? You're like a whole other human taller than me."

We laughed as we walked out of the cabin. I was beginning to feel the freedom that Mr. Thomas was telling me about. When we got to the cafeteria, Mr. Thomas motioned us both over to sit with him.

My new big bro', Tommy, said, "Hi, Mr. Thomas. You were right, this place is great."

I interrupted and asked, "Tommy, Are you new, too?"

"Yup. I am kinda new."

"Then, how are you going to be my big bro'?"

Tommy turned and mimicked a punch at my shoulder, saying, "Wait until you taste this food, Rashawn. I don't know how it was where you came from but I ain't never ate so good."

I flashed-back, and, for a minute, I thought about where I had come from, the meager meals, and the deep sadness of that darkened that place. Then, I heard someone praying for the food. Me and mom often prayed for our meals. I started to understand why mom, even as messed up as her life was, gave thanks for our food. The spark that Mr. Thomas started was now rekindling my relationship with God. It was true that He never left me. It was exactly like what Mr. Thomas had said to me in the car. The Farm was very special.

We got in line. My eyes got big as the servers gave us generous portions of food. Man, the way they piled it on, it almost seemed like they knew I was hungry. I have to admit that our food back home never looked anything like what was now on my plate. Tommy was right that Shepard's Pie and collard greens seemed like the best food I'd ever eaten. In a moment between the laugher and conversation, I thought to myself, "See, I told you so, Bo-Clyde. Real friends do exist!" I had finally found a place where I didn't have to be on guard, and I could have real friends.

Later that night, I couldn't sleep. So, I climbed down the ladder of my bunk, careful not to step on my big bro's bunk like he said. Plus, I didn't want to disturb Tommy. I went out on the front porch and just looked at the beautiful starry sky.

Suddenly, in the quiet of the night I heard a voice say, "Rashawn, Rashawn, who do you say I Am?"

I felt a comforting warmth. I fell to my knees and replied, "I know Who You are Lord. You are my Heavenly Father. My one, true Father."

Then the voice said, "Rashawn, do not fear. I am with you and soon I will send someone to be your earthly father."

Tears fell from my eyes, and I said, "Please forgive me, Father, for being so angry at You."

"Rashawn, my son, there is nothing to forgive. I love you."

I looked to the sky and said, "I love You, too, Father. I am Yours."

Just then, Tommy came out and saw me on the floor of the front deck. He turned to go back in as to not disturb my prayers.

I stopped him by asking, "Would you stay with me for a little while, big bro'?"

"Sure, what do you want to talk about?"

"Tell me what do you see when you look into the sky?"

"Lil' bro', that's easy. I see the works of our Heavenly Father's hand. We've got a good Father."

We just sat for about an hour, staring into the night, looking at the sky and talking. We fell asleep on the front deck and were awaken by the sun.

ADOPTED

It Ain't Snitching, It's The Truth!

John 8:32: *And ye shall know the truth, and* the truth shall make you free.

Tommy:
Me and Rashawn did become the best of friends. We were like real brothers. When you saw one of us, you saw the other. Neither he nor I had any surviving blood relatives who we knew about. So, our bond grew just as deep as any brothers by blood. Looking back, I realized that was the beauty of the Farm. It wasn't uncommon for boys like me and Rashawn, being from different backgrounds, cultures, and even different ethnicities, to bond on the Farm. However, even in that harmonious haven, like in all societies, there were a vocal few that sought to sow discord and division.

There was Quinton, who insisted on being called Q. He hung out with Todd, who liked to be called Loki. Those guys loved to strut around exhibiting their tattooed arms. Their bodies were covered with Confederate flags. They even went around with their shirts off to brazenly expose their chest and belly tats of SS and Nazi swastikas. They were very bold about their bigotry and hate. It was no secret that they were against the Farm's policy of acceptance. To make matter worse, they were busy trying to gather followers. Yes, they were gang recruiting. Even in this most unlikely of places, they attempted to gain power and control.

Rashawn:
Later, my big bro', Tommy, told me all about his encounter with the white supremacist guys. Meanwhile, I had my hands full with a few black militants--Ricky, who preferred to be called Stacks, and Harold, who insisted that everyone call him X. Ricky had two teardrops tattooed on his face. The two teardrops were subtle hints that he had been involved with two murders. Harold had a skull with crossbones in an X on his neck--a clear suggestion that he too was a deadly person. These two wannabe gangsters, in their new-life opportunity, just could not leave the street life in the city behind. So, now, they were busy trying to bring that lifestyle to the Farm. They also, not so secretly, were trying to recruit followers. Trying to recruit black kids. They, too, were trying to gain power.

Tommy:
Every time Q and Loki caught me alone without Rashawn, they would try to pressure me into joining their little gang.

I would try to put them off by saying, "Hey fellas, no disrespect but I had enough of that back in my old neighborhood. Here at the Farm, I'm looking for something different. I'm actually looking for a new life."

ADOPTED

They would, in turn, warn me about the deadly dangers of being a "race traitor." Then, on top of that, they would threaten me because of my friendship with my lil' bro', Rashawn. But what they had no way of knowing, was that in the few weeks that I had lived on the Farm, this new life had helped me find God and find my voice. I no longer lived in fear. I was no longer that kid, hiding in the trailer park under an old lady's trailer.

One day, I surprised myself when Q and Loki cornered me alone and tried to pressure me with threats about the old "race traitor" thing.

But, instead of being fearful, I got bold, and, with a confident smile, I replied, "Hey dudes, there's only one race being betrayed here, and that's the human race. It's being betrayed by people like y'all. Y'all just hate for the sake of hating. By the way, Rashawn is not just my friend, dudes, he's my brother! How y'all like that?"

I walked away with my head held high. But deep down inside I was still concerned because I knew these guys weren't going to stop. It was clear that they were becoming more and more dangerous. I thought about the gang back home, the Demon Venom. This could be the start of how Q and Loki could possibly gain the power they needed. They, too, could rise to the level of power they needed to be just as deadly and dangerous as the Demon Venom. I had firsthand knowledge of how that scenario could play out. Still, I dared not tell the staff because, since my days back in the trailer park, I was trained not to be a snitch. However, I would soon learn a valuable lesson from my lil' bro' Rashawn about the difference between snitching and reporting.

Rashawn:

It wouldn't be long before my big bro', Tommy, and me would find ourselves in a dangerous confrontation right here in the safest place we had ever lived, the Farm.

While Tommy and me were doing some chores together, Stacks and X walked right up to me. X came the closest. When he greeted me with a fist-bump, I was thinking that everything is going to be cool.

But then, right in front of my big bro', Tommy, in a gruff and menacing voice, X, with his head tilted to the side, asked, "Why you always hanging out with that white dude? Come on over to our side; be with your brothers."

I had finally, had enough! With cowboy western showdown music playing in my head, I slowly turned to face him. I had a frown on my face, my eyes were narrowly squinted. As tall as I am with my shoulders squared and broadened, I towered over both X and Stacks. My chest was touching X's nose.

Then, in my best "hero versus villain" voice, I slowly said, "Check this out, and don't get it twisted, I'm not your brother, and y'all certainly ain't mine. Being a brother goes way deeper than skin color. Tommy's been my brother since day one. The first day that I met him, we became brothers for life. He's a good friend and our friendship has nothing to do with loyalties to one group of people plotting on another. Good and evil has no color. I recognize good when I see it and I recognize evil when I see it. What y'all are trying to do is evil. By the way, only cowards like you guys try to mob up with evil intensions against other people. Are you fellows really alright with that? Be brave for once in your life. Be on the side of good and be constructive."

Stacks put on his mean-mug face, swelled up his chest, took a timid step closer to me, and shouted, "How you gonna call us cowards, bro'?"

Cool as a cucumber, I doubled down, and said, "Not only am I calling you cowards, but I'm reporting this incident to Mr. Will. I'm going to tell him about this whole conversation."

Stacks smiled showing his gold teeth, "Oh, so you snitching now? You're gonna to be a punk and snitch on us? You do know what happens to snitches."

I knew what to do next to be the most effective. So, I closed the distance between us and with my chest pushing on his nose, I backed Stacks up two steps, then stopped. Now we were "mano-a-mano", hand to hand. Smiling I said calmly, "Why don't you tell me all about what happens to snitches?"

Both he and X were taken by surprise. They lowered their heads. They stopped making staring-eye contact with me and decelerated their aggression. When there was no response, I knew I had what we used to call in the streets, 'chumped' them. I had called their bluff.

So, while I had their attention, I continued, "Let me give y'all an education. Let's say we were all involved in a crime and you guys got away but I got caught. If I was a coward like you cats and couldn't take my lumps, and so that I could get a lighter sentence, I would tell the cops how to catch y'all. That would be snitching. But you boys know that, you do it all the time. Here's the difference in this situation: me and Tommy, we're on the Farm's side. The Farm has fed us, and the Farm has put a roof over our heads. It's doing way more than you two bums could ever do for anybody! The Farm has a 'way better plan for our lives than y'all do. Why would I join up with you? What have you got to offer me but trouble? Loyalty is one of my strengths and I would be disloyal to our friends on the Farm if I were to keep this quiet. Fellas, you've run into the wrong person today. I'm the guy who is trying to follow Farm rules. Don't get it twisted, when I turn y'all in, that's what's called reporting, not snitching."

My big bro', Tommy, chimed in, "Yeah, when you see Rashawn or me, you see Mr. Will. You're either with the Farm or why are y'all even here?"

It was clear that the boys wanted to fight us, but it was equally clear that they knew they couldn't win. So, they just turned and walked away, leaving in their wake a bunch of choice obscenities.

All the while this was happening, none of us boys were aware of the fact that Mr. Will saw and heard everything on one of the Farm's security cameras. Later, Tommy and I would discover that the Farm had secret cameras installed in the most unnoticeable places for security reasons. The place of our encounter was one of the areas covered, and for the safety of the Farm, this certainly was a security matter.

That evening after dinner, Tommy and I sat on the front porch of our cabin. We had had a long day. It was filled with difficult challenges, but it was so good. I remember we looked up at the night sky and like almost always, it was so filled with stars, we could even see the Milky Way. Both Tommy and I were filled with gratitude. We knew that we had been rescued. This place, the Farm, was a much better place to live than either of us had ever dreamed would be possible. We talked about everything that was happening and things that we dreamed would happen. We could have talked all night.

Finally, Tommy asked me, "Rashawn, what do you think we ought to do about the creeps who tried to make you join their gang?"

Thinking about his safety, I mistakenly replied, "Tommy, I'm going to try to keep you out of this mess but I've got to tell Mr. Will. Like I said, we want to be on the Farm's side. There's no need for you to risk getting involved."

Then, I stuck my big foot even further in my mouth, "You just stay safe; it's got nothing to do with you."

What I wasn't aware of in that moment, was that the word 'safe' would trigger my big bro', Tommy, into a flashback to his hiding place in the trailer park. In a flash, he revisited the conversation with Charlie when he said to her, "I want to stay here, where it's safe." In that conversation she had made Tommy realize that he had to take action, because safety ain't easy, and freedom ain't free.

Tommy came back from his thoughts just in time to hear me foolishly say, "Besides, nobody's trying to force you to be in a gang."

I wasn't trying to hurt my big bro's feelings. It was then that he helped me to realize how my words had affected him.

CHARLES LEE KNUCKLES

Tommy replied, in an overly loud voice, "Oh, you think just because I'm short nobody wants me in a gang?"

I tried to say, "No-no that's not..."

But he wouldn't let me continue before he pointed his finger at me and shouted. "I've got news for you, big man! Just the other day some white supremacist tried to jump me into their crew. So there!"

Surprised and confused, I tried to defuse the situation by saying, "Cool your jets, 'Big Bro'. Why didn't you tell me that they tried pushing up on you like that?"

But that just made things worse. Tommy, with his eyes wide, looked up at me and moved his head back and forth with every word, "So now you think I can't handle myself, lil' bro'?"

Then, as suddenly as Tommy had exploded, he calmed down. He continued in a quieter voice, "I don't know why I didn't tell you Rashawn I guess I was trying to handle it by myself. And I did, I handled it. Well, I've handled it so far. I know them boys ain't through scheming, yet. By the way lil' bro', I've never heard snitching explained like you did today. I wish I had said that to those dudes that tried to pressure me. What do you think we should do?"

"Tommy, first thing in the morning, together, we're going to go to Mr. Will and report everything that's happened."

We looked at each other, then, smiling, we said in unison, "And that ain't snitching." We laughed and talked until it was time to turn in.

The next morning, right after breakfast, we knocked on Mr. Will's office door. Mr. Will invited Tommy and me in and directed us to sit. As if he didn't know what was going on, he asked, "What's up guys?"

"Tommy and me started speaking almost in a rhythm at the same time. Surprisingly, we were saying almost the same exact words. "Mr. Will, we've got a problem!"

Mr. Will took a second and then asked, "You guys do this all the time?"

"What do you mean?" we asked, again the same words at the same time.

"Do y'all always talk at the same time?"

Tommy and me looked at each other and then laughed.

Then I asked, "Tommy, do you want to go first?"

Tommy replied, "Sure why not? Mr. Will, some punk gang dudes are trying to recruit us into their gangs."

Mr. Will asked, "Oh, so there's more than one gang?"

This time I answered, "Yeah, my big bro' got hit on first by some white supremacist creeps. Then, I got approached by some black militant creeps."

Suddenly, Mr. Will had a strange look on his face. We were starting to think that maybe it was because he didn't believe us. We stared at Mr. Will waiting for him to reply. It seemed like for a few seconds he was stuck on pause.

Then Mr. Will turned to me first and slowly asked, "Who, is your 'Big Bro'?' Rashawn, are you telling me that there's somebody else here taller than you?"

Tommy and me looked at each for a second confused.

Then I said, "Oh! No, Mr. Will, Tommy's my Big Bro'. That's what I call him because he has helped me here at the Farm from day one."

Mr. Will looked at Tommy's diminutive size next to me for a second, then he said, "That's, actually, pretty cool. So, Tommy, what do you call Rashawn?"

"He's my Little Bro', Mr. Will."

Mr. Will couldn't help himself, he laughed, and then we all laughed.

Mr. Will would later tell Tommy and me that while he was watching things happen, he had resisted the urge to intervene. After he had heard my impromptu speech to Harold and Ricky and he noticed Tommy's reaction, he was curious as to what would happen next. Mr. Will was disappointed for Ricky and Harold.

"Tommy and Rashawn, pay attention. Ricky and Harold are already packed and they are on their way back to the group home. They probably will end up in someplace worse than Juvie because of their desire to be hateful. They wanted you to join up with them just to create havoc. I've got to say, boys, because of your courageous reporting, the Farm is safer. Now, Tommy, I think I know the two guys you're talking about, but are you brave enough to identify them for me?"

My brother, Tommy, stood up with his back straight, he said, "Watch me! Come-on, Mr. Will!"

I was so proud of Tommy, as we all walked out of the office, I also straightened my shoulders. The three of us strolled across the courtyard, straight and tall. Tommy took the lead and, boy, was he strutting. I think Tommy was eager to prove his courage against evil. The walk to the cafeteria seemed shorter than normal.

ADOPTED

Tommy marched right up to both Q and Loki. With his head held high he pointed to them. "And here's your guys, Mr. Will, him and him."

Mr. Will took all four of us to his office where he interviewed the boys, with Tommy and me not only present, but sitting on his side of the table. I don't know if Tommy and I have ever been prouder. We were on the side of what was good and right. I think that we all were surprised that Quinton and Todd not only admitted everything, but they were boastful. As a matter of fact, they were even bold enough to accused Will along with my brother, Tommy, of being race traitors.

Loki, with his finger pointing, said to Mr. Will and Tommy, "Why would you two sit with the likes of him?"

Mr. Will had heard enough, especially when they started insulting his wife, Mrs. Rennie, because of her color. Then, the boys boldly added that it wasn't too late for Tommy and Mr. Will to align themselves with the right side.

Mr. Will looked them in the eyes, "Unfortunately, I'll have to send you boys back to the group home. What you're doing is against everything we stand for here at the Farm."

Then Q replied, "That's alright, we've already got soldiers planted here." Giving Tommy a menacing stare, Q remarked, "One day soon, our people are gonna put things right with you, Little Tommy boy."

I put my arm over my brother Tommy's shoulder and said, "They will have both of us to deal with if they try anything with my brother!"

Mr. Will told Tommy and me that when he had watched the video of things happening between us and Harold and

Ricky, he was curious as to what would happen next. Mr. Will did admit that he wanted to see how Tommy and me would handle ourselves. As it turned out, he was very pleased with us. He let us know that, although we were too new in the program, he was always scouting out new leaders. He went on to explain that Farm Hands, which were the crew leaders, received and wore these really cool blue t-shirts with 'Farm Hand' printed over the pocket square. Farm Hands were responsible for showing the new boys how to swim, ride horses, row boats, and supervise the archery events. I looked at Tommy, and he looked at me, and shrugged his shoulders.

I said, "Mr. Will, I don't know about my big bro', Tommy, but I don't know how to do none of that stuff."

Tommy laughed, "I don't know how to do none of that stuff either, lil' bro'."

Will smiled and said, "That's not unusual. Intercity boys like you rarely get the chance to do the things that you boys will learn to do here on the Farm. You both will learn it all, but you'll start off by cleaning the stables."

Tommy chimed in, "Mr. Will, help us to understand. You mean our big reward is that we get to shovel horse poop?"

Mr. Will laughed as he walked away, "I trust you boys will get this very important job done right. Let's git 'er done, boys."

I yelled back, "What do you mean 'let's'? You gonna help, Mr. Will?

We all laughed, and off we went to clean the stables. Later, Mr. Will would tell us again that he was proud of us in how we stood up to Ricky, Harold, Quinton and Todd.

Tommy and I could see that Mr. Will was sad because those four boys had missed the opportunities that the Farm could give them. Strangely enough, my big bro' and I were sad for them as well. Later that night, I told Tommy that I thought God's Holy Spirit was working on us, helping us to see things more clearly. Tommy totally agreed with me. He could feel it too. We were becoming the men God had designed us to be; reversing the curse of what life had done. We were stronger as a team. We took our Bibles out and read one of our favorite stories--the story of Saul at the Damascus Road. We thought that if people like Quinton, Todd, Ricky, and Harold could have the same experience as Saul at the Damascus Road, that they could change. So, that was our prayer for that night.

CHARLES LEE KNUCKLES

Thomas Wright

Ephesians 4:2,32:
"Be completely humble and gentle; be patient, bearing with one another in love. Be kind and compassionate to one another, forgiving each other, just as in Christ God forgave you."

When an old woman rebuked him for his conciliatory attitude toward the South, which she felt should be "destroyed" after the Civil War, Abraham Lincoln replied, "Madam, do I not destroy my enemies when I make them my friends?"

    Rashawn and I would discover that the consequences of our so-called, "putting things right day", would come sooner than we thought. About a week after Q's ominous threat, Rashawn and I were walking with a group of kids along a steep river bank. The Farm had many trails to explore. I think we boys liked this trail because it has a high element of excitement and danger. It had been raining for a few days. This was the first dry day with good weather. The trail took skill to navigate, so it made us feel like a special army division on a mission. You know how young boys' imaginations run. It was heart-pounding to see that the rushing river was swollen high above its normal level. The rapids were so loud that we could hardly hear each other talking.

Suddenly, over the noise of the rapids, I heard my brother Rashawn shout, "Look out Tommy!"

I looked around just in time to see one of the boys running at me. His hands were stretched out towards me. It was clear that his intentions were to shove me into the rapids. Back then, I was a quick little fella. Just as smooth as you please, I sidestepped him perfectly and he fell face first over the embankment. Just as he was sliding down the embankment towards the rapids, he felt a hand on his ankle. It was Rashawn. He had rushed forward to rescue me but when he saw the other kid going over, he grabbed him instead. What you've got to understand about my lil' bro' Rashawn, is that it is just in his nature to help people, anybody in distress, even at the risk of danger. Even though this kid was trying to kill me, there was Rashawn, and his first thought was to save the boy that he hardly knew.

Rashawn was holding on to the kid's ankle as tight as he could, but he tripped over a rock. Now, Rashawn's body was sliding down the muddy embankment, as well.

The boy who intended to shove me was yelling, "Help me I can't swim."

At that time, none of us inter-city kids could swim and to make things worse, the rapids were way too strong for even an accomplished swimmer. We didn't stand a chance of survival in those rushing waters. I'm not proud of what I did next.

I yelled, "Let him go Rashawn, save yourself! You're going to go in with him!"

Rashawn yelled back, "I've got him. I can't just let him go!"

I decided right then that I wasn't going to lose my brother. So, I dove to the ground and with one hand grabbed Rashawn's right ankle and my other I tried to hang on to a tree trunk. The tree trunk was too slippery and my hand just slipped off. Just as we slipped downward, I hooked my one leg around the small tree trunk.

Rashawn yelled back, "Tommy, what the heck are you doing? You can't swim either. Let go, at least one of us will make it!"

Without thinking I yelled back, "Hell no! Where you go, I go! I ain't letting you go, Little Bro'. We'll figure out this swimming thing if we hit the water."

Inch by inch, all three of us were slowly sliding into the river. I said some kind of prayer as I felt pain in my leg. It was apparent that my grip on the tree was slipping. Suddenly, just as I thought that this was it, I felt a strong hand grab my belt start pulling me back. Then, much to our surprise, we were all moving in reverse, toward safety. I took a quick peep behind me to see our rescuer. It was Mr. Will, face red from the strain. His lips pursed with determination, and his cheeks puffed, filled with air. He seemed to make a grunt of power with each step backwards. In my mind, right then, I visualized Mr. Will as a superhero to the rescue. A real live superhero was pulling all three of us back on top of the embankment. That day, Mr. Will rescued all three of us. He saved our lives.

ADOPTED

On the bank of the river, returned safely to the trail, we boys were completely muddy. More importantly, we were all alive and safe. Saved from a near death experience, we all started hugging each other and thanking each other. It was like we almost forgot that this kid had tried to kill me.

Mr. Will was still catching his breath. Then, in between panting, he asked, "So, are you young men going to explain your little shenanigans here?"

We looked at each other and then just looked down at the ground and said one by one, "Sorry Mr. Will."

Although Mr. Will did not know the severity of what had just happened, he could recognize that we weren't ready to fess up yet. So, he just walked away, shaking his head and mumbling something inaudible under his breath.

Then, the kid who tried to push me into the river said to Rashawn, "I was trying to hurt your friend for being a race traitor like Q told me to do. Why did you save me? Why wouldn't you just let me fall? Why didn't y'all tell Mr. Will and get me kicked out?"

Rashawn answered his question with a question, "What's your problem? Why would you hate my big brother so much that you would try to do that to him?"

The kid looked like he had just got hit with the greatest mystery of the world. Instead of focusing on what he had just tried to do to me, he was stunned by the fact that Rashawn was black and I was white and we considered each other brothers.

He asked Rashawn, "Whoa! You're black and he's white, you're tall and he's short. So, how can he be your big brother?"

I spoke next, "So, did Q told you to kill me?"

He looked confused, "No, he just told me to hurt you and I never thought that pushing you in the river would kill you. I was just trying to teach you a lesson. I'm so sorry. I didn't think about not being able to swim until I slipped and fell. I knew that I couldn't swim but I didn't think that you couldn't swim."

Rashawn and I looked at each other. It seemed like we were both on the same page and ready to forgive the guy.

So, I said to him, "Dude, none of that trash those guys were telling you is true. They were setting you up to do their dirty work. You would have caught all the trouble while they go free. Look dude, we'll be your friends if you stop hating us for no good reason. You don't even know us yet. I'm Tommy, this is my brother, Rashawn. What's your name?"

"My name is Richard, but all of my friends just call me Richie."

I shouted, "Come on, Richie, while we're already muddy let's hunt for fishing bait, then I'll race both of you scrubs back to camp."

As muddy as we were, all three of us boys ran off together, laughing, and ready for adventure. That day, I think that we taught Richie a valuable lesson—that life is lived better without hate.

Rashawn and I had our first horseback ride at the Farm. We rode trails with other inexperienced riders. That was when we met an unusual man named David Wright. We had no clue that one day he would become our dad. As we rode, we discovered that it was also Mr. David's first horseback ride. It surprised us that an adult could be just as inexperienced

ADOPTED

as us kids. Rashawn and I liked it that Mr. David was learning just like us. It made us feel like we weren't so unusual.

It turns out that Mr. David was the father of Ms. Rennie, Mr. Will's lady friend that was staying on the Farm. Mr. David seemed angry with Mr. Will at first. When you come from the streets like me and Rashawn, no matter how they try to hide it, we could tell when a person is on the edge. It seemed like Mr. David needed somebody to talk to, so Rashawn and me hung out with him, all day. We saw him change that day; he was a whole new Mr. David. Mr. David was a little shaky on that horse, but so were Rashawn and me. Together, Rashawn, Mr. David, and I, learned a lot that day. We even learned how to handle bows and arrows. Mr. David got a bullseye and did a silly dance. Rashawn and I decided that we really liked Mr. David, so we hung out with him the whole time he visited the Farm.

One time, he literally saved my life. When I was showing off a bit, I fell into the river. Mr. David jumped right in and rescued me. Truth be told, soon after the day he rescued me, the Wright family also rescued both Rashawn and me when he and his wife, Ms. Susan, adopted us. Now, we call them Mom and Dad. Man, does that feel good.

Later, Rashawn and I learned how to swim. We learned how to row a boat, and how to fish. We learned about good food. Most importantly, we learned that regardless of what anyone thought, Rashawn and I are brothers, and now we had a mom and dad, a sister and another brother. We had finally found family.

Later, dad would say that the Farm was a magical place where we boys could be boys and could learn to live free of our fears. Dad, mom, Rennie and Jeff, found out about the Farm when Rennie read an article about dad's grandfather's death. When dad and his daughter, Rennie, came to the Farm, they met this amazing young man named Will.

Dad did not want to like Will at first, but Rennie almost instantly fell in love with him. At the same time, Will fell in love with Rennie. Their love could not be stopped. Try as he might, dad could not derail what was happening between the Will and Rennie. Dad was powerless over what was unfolding right before his eyes.

Then, something happened to dad, and he fell in love with the Farm as an orphanage. He could see everything that Will was trying to do to help young boys like Rashawn and me. It was then that dad's thoughts would change. He became happy for both his daughter, Rennie, and his future son-in-law, Will.

Whenever Will talks about the whole experience, he never mentions the trouble dad gave him in those early days.

Dad often says, "The Farm really has something special if it can change boys and bring them together. The Farm seemed to be a spiritual place that healed deep wounds and helped put things right, even with me. The relationship that Rashawn and Tommy has is really special. I like spending time with them. The day when Tommy fell from the boat, I made the commitment to not only save Tommy from drowning, but also to save both of the boys from being fatherless and from being without a family. We had to adopt them both and keep them together."

ADOPTED

The Adoption

Ephesians 1:5 *"God decided in advance to adopt us into his own family by bringing us to Himself through Jesus Christ. This is what he wanted to do, and it gave him great delight."*

"Everybody called me "Little Tommy", at the trailer park, but now everyone just calls me "Tommy", except my little bro', Rashawn, who calls me, "big bro'". I remember riding away from the Farm and looking back through dad's SUV's rear window. For me and my brother, Rashawn, life would forever be changed. Now we had a family. We had a dad, a mom, a brother and a sister. They all are amazing. And even though our new brother, Jeff, and new sister, Rennie, were mom and dad's birth kids and much older than us, Jeff and Rennie never treated us like we didn't belong. We were really family. For Rashawn and me, our wildest dreams had come true. We no longer belonged to the streets; we belonged to a good family.

Mom and dad put us in the best schools in the Brooklyn area. We were prepared for higher learning by the school at the Farm. Surprising everyone, we did well in school, although culturally we had both disadvantages and advantages. Coming from the parts of the city where we came from, experiencing what we boys had experienced, we were grateful that we performed as well as most of the kids who grew up with privilege. But we had some catching up to do. These kids were born into this upper-class environment. As a result, they exhibited a bunch of skills and training that Rashawn and I just didn't have yet. But with the help of our new adopted parents, we still excelled.

Susan, our mom, spent the most time with us, training us how to speak, how to cut food to eat that normally we might have just picked up with our hands. I mean, I get that I no longer can just pick up a steak bone when trying to get those last little morsels close to the bone, but who eats chicken drumsticks with a knife and a fork? I guess we do now!

The fact that academically we were caught up and evenly matched for our new environment, caused quite a bit of tension. Even though, when mom wasn't around, we still ate fried chicken with our hands, we were well acquainted with math skills like ratios and proportions, algebra, arithmetic with negative numbers, probability, equations and inequalities. We knew the history of the United States, England, and France. We could read fluently, analyze text and infer its message. Even with all of that, it's funny how kids can sniff out every chink in another kids' armor.

ADOPTED

Reginald Thurgood was the first to sniff out ours. Reggie lacked the courage to say anything to our faces but with the sneakiness of a snake, he spread the word that we were adopted and that our pedigree was less than desirable. At first, the barrier he placed between us and the rest of the students seemed impenetrable. We walked the halls of the school by ourselves. We ate lunch in the cafeteria by ourselves. We could see eyes looking and hear giggles. Even if they were curiously attracted, no one would dare approach us for fear of losing their standing in the school society.

But then, basketball season started and my brother, Rashawn, broke the barrier set up by Reggie, with his dominance in the sport. Rashawn, almost single handedly, changed the losing record the school had in basketball into a winning record. It was like instant fame--the kind of fame that even Reginald Thurgood couldn't stop. Rashawn made sure that I basked in that barrier-breaking glory with him by including me in everything he did. My brother did not let fame go to his head. He never left me out of anything. He let everybody know that I was his brother. He gave me credit for things I had no idea I was doing. After a winning game, he would say things like, "I would not be here if not for my big bro', Tommy. He's the coolest guy I know."

Soon, I rose to my own notoriety, scholastically. As a matter of fact, dad let the school test me in my sophomore year of high school and I scored 1580 on the SAT and had a 4.18 GPA, testing out with a 140 IQ. The school put me in an advanced class. Everybody had a plan for my life, academically. Dad wanted both Rashawn and me to practice law. The school thought that I should be a computer engineer. I could have graduated high school in my junior year but I just wanted to be a regular kid. Mostly, I just wanted to be with my brother. Together, we had adventure after adventure."

ADOPTED

Like Father, Like Son: Rashawn

"More than anything, I, Rashawn Wright, wanted to be like my adopted dad, David Wright, a brilliant lawyer. From where I had come from, I had never seen or known a man like dad. He had his own firm that did corporate work all over the world. He was very successful, but respectful, and kind. I imitated everything about him that I could. He had to notice my admiration but he never showed it in any way. He is a great dad.

I remember my first case; my very first legal battle. I was in high school when our math teacher was facilitating a particularly boring class. Well, it was boring to most of the kids, but since I struggled in math, I hung on to every word, and I rigorously took all the notes I could. I took "copious notes," as dad would say.

One day in class, I hadn't even noticed, but one of the kids created this massive spit-wad and threw it. The thing was so

CHARLES LEE KNUCKLES

huge that it made a smacking sound when it made contact with Mr. Greenberg's bald spot in the back of his head. The kid's bold action and the loud smacking sound drew a roar of laughter from most of the class. When Mr. Greenberg spun around in a rage, many kids were laughing, but my head was down. I was trying desperately to keep up with my notes. Mr. Greenberg took my lowered head as a sign of guilt. He walked over to my desk. I looked up at him, trying to figure out what was going on.

He grabbed my shirt collar and barked, "Come with me, young man."

This made the class roar even louder. Mr. Greenberg took the laughter as a sign that he had nabbed the right culprit. I was taller than him, so he had to let go of my collar as I followed him to the principal's office.

I sat in the reception area while Mr. Greenberg shouted at the principal about me. They called my dad. I waited in the office for a long time. Dad walked in the office, straight over to me, but the principal intercepted him.

"Mr. Wright, your son has committed a serious assault on a teacher. Rashawn totally disrupted the class by throwing an object and hitting the teacher in the head. Needless to say, we take this assault seriously and a discipline will be issued."

Dad came over to me and asked, "Did you do this, son?"

I looked him in the eyes and said, "No, dad, I didn't do it."

Dad said, "Since you know what went on, you will have to argue your case. Are you up to it?"

"Dad, if they give me a fair chance, I will win."

ADOPTED

Dad smiled a smile that said it all. He believed in me. Then, he looked at me, "Son, you will get that fair chance. I'll make sure of that. I have all the confidence in the world in you. But that won't matter unless you have confidence in yourself. Believe in yourself, son!"

Dad turned, and right then, Mr. Zimmerman asked him, "Mr. Wright, what have you to say about your son and his actions?"

"Mr. Zimmerman, my son deserves the right to defend himself. He will speak for himself. He should have the right to face his accuser and give his side of the story."

Principal Zimmerman seemed very confident. He looked dad in the eyes and said, "OK if that's what you want, I'll call Mr. Greenberg in to give you his account."

"Yes, please call him in. But he won't be dealing with me, he will be dealing with my son. I'm just here to see that my son gets a fair shake. Then, whatever the outcome, we'll accept it."

Mr. Zimmerman had his secretary call Mr. Greenberg. Mr. Greenberg entered the office with anger still in his eyes. As soon as he took a seat, I stood up and walked in front of Mr. Greenberg, I tried to imitate my dad and how I had seen him act in court. I took a couple steps away and then, turned.

"Mr. Greenberg, did you see me throw the alleged spit wad?"

Mr. Greenberg with indignance, gruffly replied, "What do you mean alleged? Here's the spit-wad right here!"

I used a strategy I'd seen dad use. and I took a second, then I calmly said, "Mr. Greenberg, I'm not alleging that the spit-wad does not exist. It's very evident that it does and it's equally clear that you were assaulted with it. I'm alleging the accusation against me. Now, Mr. Greenberg, did you see me throw the spit-wad?"

"No, my back was turned when you hit me."

I looked over at dad, he had a big smile on his face that gave me a boost in confidence.

"Mr. Greenberg, if you did not see me throw it, then why would you think that I threw the spit-wad?"

Mr. Greenberg increased his fiery attitude and pointed his finger at me, "Look, Rashawn, when I turned, you were the only student that had his face down, buried in the textbook, like a guilty person."

I took a second, and then replied, "Hmmm, my face was buried in my book you say?"

"Yes, like a guilty person."

"Mr. Greenberg, do you remember what you were teaching at the time?"

"Yes, it was the formula for converting Celsius to Fahrenheit."

"May I show you my notebook, Mr. Greenberg?"

Then, I turned to Mr. Zimmerman, "Mr. Zimmerman, I offer exhibit A. Mr. Greenberg would you read the last written notation please?"

Mr. Greenberg read my notes, "To convert temperatures in degrees Celsius to Fahrenheit, multiply by 1.8 (or 9/5) and add 32". As Mr. Greenberg read my notes the expression on his face changed.

Later, dad confessed that at that point he almost jumped out of his chair and screamed, "That's my boy!!!" But both he and I remained calm as I finished my summation.

"Mr. Greenberg, do you think that it would be possible for me to have such detailed notes, and create and throw spit-wads at the same time?"

Mr. Greenberg looked up from my notebook and said, "I have to admit, these notes are impeccable. They are almost verbatim the very text that I taught."

Just to add a little drama in my summation, I turned away, looked upwards, and asked, "Mr. Greenberg can you now admit that I might have had my head lowered in my notebook for the simple purpose of taking notes and it had nothing to do with guilt?"

Mr. Zimmerman said, "I've heard enough. Mr. Wright you have our most humble apologies for calling you down here, sir."

He stood ready to shake my dad's hand, when dad said, "Sir, more than me, you owe my son that apology. Both of you owe him an apology".

The two men turned to face me. Mr. Zimmerman repeated his apology to me. Mr. Greenberg also apologized. Then Mr. Greenberg asked, "Rashawn, who did throw the spit-wad?"

"Mr. Greenberg, you saw my notes. Your attention was on the blackboard, my attention was on taking notes as thorough as I could. How would I know that any more than you?"

I had my suspicions about who actually did throw the spit-wad, but if I was to be a lawyer like my dad, I would have to have actual proof. Nevertheless, I had won my first legal battle. Dad was so proud of me.

I could see it in his eyes when he took me by my shoulders, and said, "Son, you've got what it takes to be a really good lawyer. I'm very proud of the way you handled yourself like a top notched professional."

Later, I did find out who threw the spit-wad, through his own confession. It turns out that it was Ricky, one of the jocks. Ricky thought he didn't need the class, so, in order to entertain himself, he threw the spit-wad. I did not share my findings with the faculty. I didn't want to make enemies in class, besides Ricky would just have denied it.

After that day, Mr. Greenberg treated me with a bit more respect. He had always addressed me as "Mr. Wright," but now it sounded different. All the other teachers who just called me Rashawn, treated me more like a serious student. From that time on, they looked at my work with a greater respect. They started encouraging me when I was struggling, and celebrated my work when I did well. Even though I was a minority in the school, I no longer felt like a minority. I was Rashawn.

Even though I might not have had an IQ as high as my big bro', Tommy, I now could see that I was at least in the ballpark. Academically, I, too, belonged here. I was not just another jock.

ADOPTED

The Big City and Little Tommy

Our dad, David Wright, was born in New York, in the Brooklyn Park Slope neighborhood, to Eli and Viola Wright. Eli and Viola bought the stately home that mom and dad still owned. Rashawn and I now lived in that very same home with all of its history. Dad and mom love everything about New York, from the townships to the cities and boroughs.

New York is a big city and as scary as it might sound to live here, dad will tell you that he rarely felt unsafe. Most of that is to granddad Eli's credit. He was successful at work and was able to keep his family in safe neighborhoods. At the height of grandpa Eli's success, he bought the mansion in Park Slope.

New York State has a population of almost twenty million people and well over nine million of that population is in New York City. Dad would laughingly say, "I was never alone." Then he would get serious and give us these instructions.

CHARLES LEE KNUCKLES

"The trick is to choose carefully what crowd you associate with. You've got to have good New York instincts. Always be in good company, stick to the main street, and most importantly, never, ever act like a tourist. I taught Jeff and Rennie these strategies for living in the Big Apple and now I've got you two beautiful, young boys and you are from a small town in Virginia. It is my responsibility to keep you safe, too."

I don't know if dad and mom always remembered that Rashawn and me already had street smarts.

Early in the adoption, it was hard for me to adjust. Sometimes I suffered, not from clinical depression, but you could say that I was low in my spirit. I have some really bad memories. I lived a rough life back in the trailer park, and some tragic things happened back there. Now, I have a new mom and a new dad, who are wonderful to both myself and Rashawn. Everything should be great. Still, I would, on occasions, drift back into thoughts of my biological mom and dad. At times, I could still hear that horrible explosion that took them.

With a new model of masculinity and fatherhood in David, sometimes just thinking about the things my biological dad would make me do, would suddenly make me break down and cry. David, my new dad, would worry about me. So, on occasions, he would make time to spend a whole day with just him and me.

Dad would lift my spirits and make me feel special when he would take me shopping for new sneakers or a special football or soccer jersey. Often, with his hand on my shoulder, we would stop and window shop before going into the store.

ADOPTED

I'll never forget this one day in particular, as we stood looking into the store window, Dad asked, "Tommy what do you think about that top? Is it fly? Fly is what you kids say these days?"

"No dad, fly is definitely out, we say it's 'lit' now, and that top is definitely lit."

In the reflection of the store window, I noticed a lady talking to a man and pointing her finger at us. Dad was so focused on making my day that he was completely oblivious of what was going on behind us, but my street senses were tingling.

"Dad, look but don't look right now. See the reflection in the window? There's a lady pointing at us and gathering a crowd behind us."

Dad was not stealth at all. He immediately turned around, and upon noticing the lady and her crowd, he said, "What's all this about? Something troubling you folks?"

The white lady was now even more emboldened because she was standing between the two huge white men she had recruited. She said, "Why are you holding that white kid hostage? Are you some kind of perverted monster that thinks he can just grab up a kid in broad daylight?"

"Look lady, I don't know why it would be any of your business, but this is my son. We are out for a day to ourselves. So, if you don't mind..."

Dad went to turn back to the store window when one of the big men approached us, sticking his hand out to me, saying, "Kid come with me, You're safe now."

I started to freak out. Already, I had worst-case scenarios running in my head. Even though I am not a crier, the tears were flowing down my cheeks. Seeing and misjudging my tears, the men moved in, grabbed and wrestled my dad to the ground, and held him down on the dirty New York pavement. Pinned to the street, and even though my dad was helpless with the man's knees in his chest, dad was worried about my safety.

"Don't worry Tommy, the police will be here soon. Don't be afraid, this will all be straightened out soon."

At this point, they started to punch and kick dad. Two more men joined in the chaos, and with the lady screaming and cheering them on, they went into an even more violent frenzy. By the time the police arrived, dad was already bloody and semi-conscious. Instead of arresting the people that were assaulting dad, the biggest cop put his knee on the back of my dad's neck while another handcuffed him.

They kept saying, "Stop Resisting" while they were throwing him in a squad car.

I kept crying, and yelling, "Leave my dad alone. I want my dad."

The lady shouted, "Darn pervert has got the kid brainwashed."

The lady and two of the men gave their names and statements to the police. Then, the other men were eager to give their names and reports. They all must have thought that they were heroes and would get a hero's recognition.

But for dad and me, just that quick, our beautiful day trip had turned into a nightmare. Soon, we were both at the

ADOPTED

police station. The cops separated us without even listening to us. I kept saying, "He's my dad," but dad was semi-conscious and could not speak for himself. I don't know where they took dad, but they had me in a little room. I was wondering what would happen next. In walked a police officer and a caseworker from CPS.

She asked, "Hi, what's your name, son?"

I was so angry. "I'm not your son," I replied. "I have a mom and a dad and you people have just roughed up my dad and you've got him locked up for no reason."

The CPS worker gave me a smile, and asked, "Yes, we know he says he is your dad but who is he, really?"

I looked her in the eyes and said, "Lady, look at my ID. My name is Thomas Wright, my dad is David Wright, and he is an attorney. He has his own practice in Manhattan and all of you are in a lot of trouble."

For the first time since all of this mess started, someone actually heard me. She looked at my identification. Suddenly, the CPS worker's expression completely changed. Have you ever seen that look on someone's face when they suddenly realize that they have made a horrible mistake? Yeah, that was the look she had on her face.

Wide-eyed, she quipped, "Let me borrow your ID." Then, she took my ID and ran out of the room.

I remember it all as if it was yesterday. A lady police officer brought some chips and a soda and sat them in front of me with a half-hearted smile.

I said, sharply, "Look officer, I don't want your chips or soda. I want my dad, what's wrong with you people?"

Dad was led into the room by the cops that had arrested him. He was bleeding from his forehead, his eyes were blackened, and his clothes were torn. I had never seen dad so angry, but his first concern was me.

He asked, "Tommy are you alright? Did they hurt you?"

"No dad, they just scared me something terrible. I thought that they were going to kill you. From the way they were acting, I thought I would never see you again."

Dad turned to face the officers and said their names slowly as if he was committing to memory. "Officer Bennett, and Officer O'Reilly, I'll be needing a copy of your arrest report."

And then he turned to me with his arm around my shoulder. We walked right pass them to the desk officer to retrieve dad's belongings.

Dad sued everyone involved and we ended up with five million dollars. He put two million in a trust fund for me. There I was, me, Tommy Wright, a millionaire at 15 years old. I never cared about that money. I didn't like anything about how it all went down. Later, in my faith walk with God, I was able to forgive all the people who turned dad's and my beautiful day into a nightmare.

Dad invested that money so well that it multiplied to so many million that I could hardly believe I was so rich. Sometimes over breakfast, dad would show me the Wall Street Journal. He would point to different stocks and say, "Well it looks like your stocks are doing pretty well, Tommy."

Later, when I got older and became a pastor, I gave a lot of that money away to good causes.

Dad would just smile, hug my neck, and say, "Tommy, I don't know why you give so much of your money away. It's just who you are, you give so much more than you take. Your mom and I love you so much. I know that you believe your Heavenly Father loves you even more, but He's got His work cut out if He is going to love you more than your mom and me." Then he laughed that wonderful laugh that we all loved to hear. He seemed to reserve that lovely laugh just for our family.

Life may have gotten off to a rough start for me and my brother Rashawn but God's generous love bathed us in His amazing grace.

Memories of the violence, the trauma, and confusion of my childhood followed me even in my beautiful new home, but love was more powerful. Love was shaping and molding Rashawn and me into who God had designed us to be as young men.

CHARLES LEE KNUCKLES

The Great Nerd Rescue: Rashawn

School for Tommy and me was pretty cool. Both of us were challenged when we first arrived. Not so much by the curriculum but by the culture. It's true that the rich live differently than the poor. We weren't poor anymore, but we knew poverty first hand. Dad made sure that we had everything the other kids had, all the latest clothes, and all the latest gear. Our laptops were insane!

    Even in this culture of rich kids, they had their tough guys. They quickly realized both Tommy and me could hold our own with them. The novelty of Tommy being white and me black wore off quickly when people saw that the bond of our brotherhood went deeper than many blood relatives. It wasn't long before I was recruited by the jocks because of my height and athletic abilities. Even though we both were measured to be above average intelligence, Tommy was next-level smart. His IQ was genius level, so naturally the smart kids drafted him in with their group. We hung out with those other kids but we enjoyed hanging out with each other much more. So, there was tension. The smart kids would try to get Tommy to hang out with them exclusively and ignore me, his jock brother, and the jocks would try to get me to not associate with my nerd brother. Surprisingly, it was not about black or white, but just about the jocks vs. nerds.

One day, a group of jocks came up with a ridiculous and reckless scheme to harass those who they called, among other names, "the nerd kids." I not only had an affinity for nerds, but then, there was my brother, the king of the nerds. The jock's plan was to set off a smoke bomb near the computer class and pull the fire alarm. While the nerds were out of the classroom, a couple of the jocks would smear peanut butter all of the computer keyboards including the nerds' personal laptops.

Immediately, I just flat out said, "I ain't doing that! That's stupid and criminal--you're talking felony-level criminal. That's thousands of dollars of equipment. At those numbers, it's definitely a felony. There's also the fact that, now that I know, I'd have to report all of you."

Ricky Dallas tried to chump me, "Oh, so you're a snitch?"

I looked him in his eyes and said, "Nope, I'm not a snitch but somebody's got to stand up against criminals. That would make you all criminals. You do know that if you do something like that, it's a serious crime. You guys are so stupid that you don't even realize that you all could get criminal records for property damage on a felony level."

Then, Joe Williams, the quarterback of the football team agreed with me. "OK dudes, Rashawn could be right. We don't want get criminal records for property damage."

Even Ricky Dallas gave up the idea and agreed. I walked away thinking everything was ok and that the prank was called off. But sadly, I wasn't even close. Instead, the jocks came up with a different plan, and this time, since I was considered a snitch, I wasn't included in the planning stage of the plot. This time, the plan was different and much more personal against the nerds. This time it would be a physical assault on all the boys considered to be nerds.

The plan went into action. During class break, the jocks herded the nerds into the boys' bathroom with the false report that a top scientist was testing the pH levels of the school's water with a new device that did not need to be submerged in the water. The nerds flocked to the boys' room to see this new device and meet the scientist. Once in the bathroom, they were corralled and could not escape. The jocks had already taken most of the nerds' shirts and pants. The jocks were at the point of their nefarious scheme where they were ready to relieve the nerds of their shorts and start dunking their heads in the toilets. With the largest of the jocks blocking the bathroom door, the nerds were trapped in the boys' room and final humiliation was about to take place. For the finale, the nerds were to be made to run through the halls soaked in toilet water, and past everyone, without their underwear.

Everything was working to plan for the jocks, that is, until I heard about what they were doing. I knew that my brother would be there. I ran as fast as I could. When I burst past the jock guards into the boys' room, I saw that the jocks had a group of the smart kids lined up by the stalls in their underwear. They were ready to dunk them and flush the toilets. Many were in their underwear, that is all except my brother, Tommy.

He was in the fight of his life with a jock named Kenny. Surprisingly enough, Tommy was holding his own. Then, Ricky Dallas stepped in and tried to hold Tommy's arms. Ricky never saw my punch coming. I walked up to him and said, "Hey Ricky!" And when he turned to see me, I dropped him with a solid right cross, right over his shoulder and into his jaw. Yes, it was a sucker-punch, but I knew that I had to have shock value on my side. I needed to make an intense move like that punch because Tommy and I were outnumbered.

Kenny turned from Tommy to come at me, and Tommy tripped him. Kenny was flat on the floor with Tommy's foot between his shoulders pinning him to the floor. At that moment, my brother Tommy looked so heroic, standing in victory, with his foot on the giant jock, like David conquering Goliath. Tommy looked over at me with a smile and said "Little brother, you ready to kick some butt?"

We now had the jock's full attention. Standing side by side, it was me and Tommy who now blocked the door.

Tommy said, "Give them back their clothes and we will let you get out of here without getting busted up! Starting with this punk I've got on the floor. One twist of my foot and I'll separate Kenny's vertebrae." It was a bluff Tommy had just thought it up on the fly. But it seemed to be working.

I said, "And here you all thought that my big brother was just another nerd. How are all you so-called jocks going to explain getting beat down and put in wheelchairs by a nerd?"

Kenny, from the floor, sacred to death, said, "It's over, guys. Don't let this crazy maniac break my neck! Just let them all go".

Tommy and I both laughed with so much crazy confidence that the jocks, thinking that we were crazed killers from the ghetto, started returning the smart kids their clothing, even helping them get dressed. One by one, the jocks left the bathroom squeezing by us with one eye on Kenny under Tommy's foot and one eye on our fists.

After they all left, Tommy lifted his foot and told Kenny, "Go on creep, git!"

In tears, Kenny scurried out the door.

From then on, the Wright brothers had a different kind of reputation. One of being tough but fair. When there were disputes, people sought out Tommy and me to negotiate solutions. Dad taught us so much about being lawyers that all the negotiating seemed natural. Also, dad taught us how to communicate so well that a group of students convinced me to run for class president, and I won.

ADOPTED

Money Can't Call Me Honey: Tommy and Judy

After the whole bathroom adventure went legendary, I was the first nerd to be respected by the jocks. I must admit, I loved the status. Girls started flirting with me. Imagine that, me, Tommy Wright, a chick magnet. I still have to laugh at the thought. However, I was way too busy to be distracted. Nevertheless, distraction did come into my life-- a blonde-haired, blue-eyed distraction named Judith Ann Kelly.

Our herd of students thinned out dramatically when it came to the special, 11th grade calculus class. I could not help but notice her--she is so beautiful, and competitive. She and I seemed to compete for perfect grade scores. We also both had a thirst for being the first to solve the hardest equations in our calculus group discussions. Sometimes, I would be the first to finish, and sometimes she would be the first to finish.

I thought, "How in the world could someone be so beautiful and yet so smart." To top things off, Judy loved and excelled in basketball. Judy Kelly was an incredible three-point shooter. She literally won games for the girls' team with her three-point shots. She once told me that it was the math of basketball that got her interested in the sport. I'm not trying to be sexist, but she is fit, beautiful, and smart. Although Judy is modest, she is confident at the same time. She keeps me guessing, it's impossible to figure her out.

Judith Ann Kelly is a mystery to me--a mystery that I'm drawn to. I asked myself, "Is she out of my league?" Leave it to my brother, Rashawn, to challenge me.

He said, "The fact that you have to ask yourself if she's out of your league, big bro', means that she is definitely out of your league. But remember what dad tells us all the time, 'Shoot for the stars, the moon, and the sun!'"

What I didn't know at the time, but would discover later, was that she was wondering the very same thing. Later, Judy would tell me that she always thought I was smart, strong, and confident. I was her "stars, moon, and sun." She said that it was rare that she would meet a guy who didn't smoke, drink, do drugs, or cuss, and who always used proper English. I guess I've got dad to thank for the proper English. He insisted that Rashawn and I use correct grammar at all times.

"One day, I noticed Judy shooting hoops by herself. Her head would tilt to the side, and mouth was moving like she did when she was figuring out math. It was a beautiful thing. She was doing mathematical equations in her head with each shot. She rarely missed a shot. When she finally missed one, I rushed in and caught the rebound.

"What happened?", I asked. "Wrong arc? Not enough force? The spin?"

She looked at me for a second, and said, "Not the right arc, of course. But you knew that didn't you?"

I did a turn-around jump shot that bounced off the back of the rim. "I've never mathed out shots before but maybe I should. Maybe it would make me a better player. Want to show me?"

We spent the rest of the afternoon playing b-ball and talking. She beat me in every game but we laughed so hard, it didn't feel like a loss--it felt like a win. That was the best time I'd had in a long while. We gave up the court for a group of guys that wanted to play a full court game.

As we walked, Judy asked, "So, what's your plan, Mr. Thomas Wright?"

"Oh, so you know my last name?"

"Don't flatter yourself, Thomas, we're in some of the same classes. Of course, I know your full name. Do you know mine?"

"I could see that she was hoping I did, so I took the opportunity for a little fun. "Let me see... Oh yeah, you are in my calculus class and did I see you in Comparative Literature or was that Creative Writing? Oh, wait you are Judith Kelly, right?"

"Thomas, tell me why I should keep talking to you after that display of immaturity?"

"I don't know Judith, maybe to save my basketball game? Or maybe because I like you a lot."

She smiled, and looked me in the eyes, "You don't even know me a lot!"

"Yes, I do, Judy. You are kind. You are gentle but strong. You're smart and thoughtful. Oh, I've been paying attention."

Judy smiled, "OK, I guess that could get you a few more minutes of my time, Tommy Wright."

We took the bus and chatted so much that we almost missed her stop. Then, we chatted some more on the bus stop bench. Finally, I walked Judy to her door. The evening ended in one of those awkward moments where we didn't know whether to shake hands, hug, or just wave goodbye, but definitely not kiss, not even a peck. Judy didn't have to set the boundaries, although I'm sure she would have if I had tried to kiss her. I had heard the men in my life talk about how to treat a lady. I'd seen the way my brother-in-law Will and my sister Rennie dated before they married. Judy was already very special to me. So, I had already decided that I was going to treat her with respect and dignity. I wasn't going to mess this up by getting ahead of myself. So, I just gave an awkward wave goodnight and like a gentleman, I waited until she was in the house to walk away.

The next day, at school, Judy and I spent practically all of our free time together. We had an instant attraction.

There came a time when the school's computer system was hit with a virus that downloaded malicious malware. Needless to say, it totally crashed the entire computer system. Since I was the most advanced computer nerd in the school, inquiring minds wanted to know if I had anything to do with it? Everyone whose computer was connected to the school's system was infected. Since my computer had gotten infected just like all the others and that seemed to be proof enough that I was not the source of the infection, I was off the hook.

Not so much for the PE teacher. An outside tech support came in and tracked down the source. It turns out that while the professor was watching porn in his office, he accidently downloaded the virus onto his computer and it invaded the whole network. The school had just cause to fire him for misuse of school property. He was responsible for the cost of replacing some of the older computers that could not be repaired, and for reprogramming the new computers. The school lost a lot of data. We students would have trouble getting our computers repaired. The whole process of making a claim and proving the damage would be time-consuming.

It was then that I came up with one of my most hairbrained ideas ever. I needed Judy to help me out. I had been with Rashawn when he played basketball in some sketchy neighborhoods. Although Rashawn, because he thought it was too dangerous, never played for money, while there I noticed others bet on games. They would bet big money, and if Judy and I could get in and win a couple grand, I could get a new laptop.

I told Judy of my plan and that it could be dangerous. She just smiled and said, "I'm in!"

I was so in the zone, I said, "Honey, now, these guys like to run roughshod over teams that come to play on their courts. If we come in for a layup, we could get hurt. All we have to do is to hang out in the three-point zone. Can you nail seven three-pointers in a row?"

Judy smiled, "Just seven? I can do more than that in a row! But wait a minute-- back-up a little! Did you just call me, 'honey?'"

I realized I had gotten too carried away and called Judy, "honey". "Oops! I'm sorry Judy, was that wrong?"

Judy had a dreamy smile, "No, not at all, but now, I almost can't wait for our first kiss."

I moved in with my lips puckered. "We can take care of that right now!"

Judy stopped me with her hand on my chest. "Hold on, tiger, I said 'almost.' You are going to have to wait, Mr. Tommy."

The whole ride to the basketball court, we strategized and planned our game. Then came our subway stop. We held hands as we walked and said a quick prayer.

When we stepped onto the blacktop basketball court, we were met with a round of laugher.

"What's up Vanilla Ice? You and Barbie lost?"

Judy spoke up first, "We may be vanilla but our money is green! We want a two-on-two challenge to twenty-one points. Only serious players need to step-up and try to win this five hundred!"

Two older guys looked us up and down and then, the tallest one said, "OK, easy money, let's do this!"

I said, "Let's see your money first".

"Come over to the car and get a look."

We exchanged glances at each other's cash, then we played. Just like I thought, they smashed the first shot with a dunk. More brute force than finesse. Then, the shorter of the two missed a three-pointer, and with my quickness, the rebound came to me. It was time for us to out-think our opponents. Luckily, Judy and I had worked out our strategy. I came driving in and they double-teamed me. Just when it looked like they were going to crush my shot, I spun and passed the ball back to Judy. I set her up twice and she made two three-pointers in a row. Then, the two ballers pressed her and she purposely miss one. She successfully made them underestimate her, and I got the rebound because they were covering her. I made a couple of shots, and then they crowded me, leaving Judy wide open. I sent the ball back to Judy and she dropped a couple more three-pointers.

Soon, the game was at 16, us, and 18, them. They tried to finish us off with a three-pointer that missed. That would have been it for us--they would have walked away with our money. I hustled and got the rebound. Judy nailed a three-pointer from the left side of the court, again. Then, with the next shot, she took the ball in on the right side of the court. Judy had purposely missed from the right side of the court, twice before.

One of the guys said, "She's got nothing on the right side of the court." So, they moved in for the rebound. Judy arched the ball so high it seemed like slow motion, then, there it was, that swish, net-slapping sound the ball makes when it goes in so smooth it barely touches net.

Immediately, the ballers, upset by the win, shouted, "Double or nothing, freakshow!"

I replied, "I don't know--we might not be able to beat you guys again. Maybe we ought to just take our winnings and leave."

That seemed to make them want us all the more. The big guy said, "But why just take the thousand, when you could possibly have two? Unless y'all are scared of a second game?"

I walked over to Judy and asked, "What do you think, honey?"

I wasn't ready for what happened next. She grabbed me by the back of my neck, pulled me in, and kissed me with a hot, steamy kiss, and then, she said, "Why not, honey?"

Stunned for a moment, I slowly turned and said, "Alright, let's go."

With her three-point game on-point and my hustle untiring, we won again.

Now, it was time for pay off. But would they pay us? They didn't have to pay us, no money had changed hands. All we had was what we came with, our five hundred dollars.

Then, we all shook hands and the shortest of the two men said, "We're not going to pull money out on the court, come over to my car."

I didn't know what to think so I told Judy to wait over by the gate, just in case she had to run.

Judy looked at me like I was crazy, "Run and leave you by yourself, the man with whom I just shared my first kiss? I thought you knew me better than that, Tommy Wright."

Judy was into the thrill of our big adventure. My emotions were all confused. I didn't know how to feel--fear, excitement, love all rolled up into one. At the same time, I had to appear calm and steady. It was awesome and scary at the same time. Judy and I walked to the car with every step shrouded in mystery.

We got to the car and the tallest guy says, "I'm just dealing with one of you. One of y'all get in the front seat and the other, wait outside."

Judy, for the first time showed a little fear. She spoke in a nervous voice, "We do everything together."

"Don't make it weird, lady. I'm not having one of y'all in my backseat while I count out this money. It's not the way I do things! Now, do what I said and everything will be cool!"

I turned to Judy and said, "I'll be alright, honey," and I got in the car.

When I sat down, he said, "You guys are pretty slick out there on that court."

I thought to myself, "Oh shoot, do they feel hustled?"

I didn't know what was going to happen next, until he pulled out his money from the console. He counted out two thousand dollars and shook my hand. "I wouldn't advise you two trying that stunt around here, again. Not everybody around here is quite as honorable as me and Jason."

I thanked him. Then, Judy and I jogged all the back to the subway station, laughing and giggling. It wasn't enough for the computer I wanted, but it was adventure. I asked Judy what was she going to do with her thousand.

She said, "Nothing! I did this for you to get yourself a new computer. I put my claim in on my computer early. My new computer is on its way. You take the money, Tommy."

CHARLES LEE KNUCKLES

Of course I refused, claiming gentlemanly status, and insisted that she take her thousand. Thanks to my big-mouthed brother, she soon found out that it all was a deception. When we got back to my house, Rashawn was by the garage, playing basketball. He invited us to shoot some hoops.

I said, "Sit down, little bro'. I've got a story to tell you."

When I was just about to begin, Judy jumped in and I'd never heard her talk so fast. Before I could say a word, she told Rashawn the whole story in what seemed like one, long sentence. When Judy ended the story with, "We did it all so that Tommy could get a new laptop, but he insisted that I take half. So we may have to do something else to get the rest of the money!"

I knew with that one long sentence I was in trouble.

Before I could stop Rashawn, he blurted out, "But bro', you're probably the only multi-millionaire kid in school. You've got millions and you're trying to get a computer with a b-ball hustle?"

Judy looked at me with shock. Before I could get out, "Let me explain", she was running down the street.

Rashawn, realizing what just happened, said, "Aw man! You didn't tell your girl? I'm sorry bro. What was you thinking and what are you going to do now?"

Quite frankly, I didn't know what I was going to do. Judy wouldn't answer my calls for a whole day. I was moping around the house like a sad pup the rest of the day. The next morning, I went over to Judy's house early. I waited on her stoop for her to leave the house for school. The door opened, and I thought she would sit with me. When Judy walked by me, she smacked me in the back of my head. As she passed by me, she quipped, "Good morning stupid."

I got up quickly to keep up. I tried to keep step, matching her stride, step by step all the way to the bus stop, while pleading my case. "Honey, I'm so sorry I didn't tell you about the money. I didn't want it to have any part in our relationship. Sometimes, I don't want it to have anything to do with my life. I wanted our love to be pure, with no influence of the money."

Judy stopped, and it seemed like so did the world. She turned and said, "Just to be clear Thomas, I'm angry at you for not trusting me. It has nothing to do with your money. But after some consideration, I can understand your paranoia about the money. I want you to know this, Thomas Wright, I don't need your money. I'm smart enough to make my own money. Besides, I fell in love with you, not your money. *Money can't call me honey!* Now, keep up, and don't make me late for my bus!"

Judy's independence and strength was magnificent to me, but ultimately it was her love that was truly epic and gave us the ability to follow our true path. Together, we could have taken Manhattan by storm. With our combined academic gifts, the backing of my dad, my millions of dollars, we could make billions. People thought that we were a perfect power couple for the corporate world. But God was calling us to ministry. I felt I was called, with Judy by my side, to pastor a church.

CHARLES LEE KNUCKLES

Love: Rashawn

In high school, I watched my brother, Tommy, and Judy fall deeply in love with each other. They seemed inseparable. I noticed that when they talked to each other, they looked deeply into each other's eyes as if they had no secrets, no barriers. They held each other's hands, walking through the halls, talking as if there was no one else there but them. Tommy and Judy were fiercely committed to one another. They didn't let anything separate them, not school gossip, not school politics, not the jealousies of any other boys or girls. It seemed like many kids were jealous of Tommy and Judy, but I wasn't jealous of my brother. I loved him too much not to want the best for him. Judy was certainly the best.

    I guess I was sort of feeling sorry for myself because I didn't have what he had in Judy. Even though I was popular, I had not found that kind of connection. Sometimes, it felt like I would never find the love of my life in this school. Oh, there were girls, but they all were interested in having me as their basketball-star trophy. I had seen enough real examples of

ADOPTED

love to know the difference between if a girl was interested in me or if it was just lust. I saw real love between Will and Rennie, my mom and dad, and now in my brother, Tommy, and Judy.

Tommy and I were more fortunate than we knew when we got adopted by dad and mom. For instance, dad was so aware of Tommy's and my emotions that, when all of this was going on, he saw that I was a little down in the dumps, and asked, "What's up, Rashawn? What's going on?"

I told him how I felt guilty about being a little jealous of Tommy and Judy. How I felt like I had lost my big bro'.

"Look, son, you are a godly young man. I assure you that God has your best interest at heart. He is generous in His thoughts of you, son. He has the perfect mate in mind for you. He's preparing you both for each other. This is all just a part of you maturing emotionally. When you meet the woman that God has waiting for you, your love together will be epic. Just be with God for now, let Him mold and shape you into the man He has designed you to be, and the young woman that He is molding and shaping to be one with you will find you at the same time that you will find her."

I smiled at dad and said, "About that shape that God's working on, dad, I'm requesting that she be tall, with long legs, fine looking, and smart." We both laughed. "I'm just putting my wish list out there, dad."

I went on to pour myself into my school work and sports. My work ethic began to shape me into who I am today. I was so fortunate to have a family that showed me love, good work ethics, and how to have fun.

In university, Tommy and I took the same majors, we both ended up with law degrees and Masters of Divinity. Dad prompted us both toward corporate law. That was the biggest money maker and besides, it was what dad's law firm practiced. I knew that I needed to make money fast to live in New York, so I studied hard to become one of the best corporate lawyers in Manhattan. Tommy, on the other hand, studied human-rights law. Dad had invested Tommy's millions, and after years, Tommy had more money than he could possibly spend in a lifetime.

Money or not, we had to work throughout school. It seems like we were probably two of the youngest paralegals in New York. Throughout university, I had the advantage of sitting in on high-level corporate cases. Later, I would assist lawyers with their case preparation and do research for them. I spent a lot of time helping lawyers with legal arguments, motions, and filing documents. Tommy did the same, but there came a time when he went from paralegal with dad's firm to becoming a legal clerk with the court. Dad was amazed with Tommy's decision. Dad expressed a little disappointment that Tommy left the firm, but at the same time, he was also encouraging.

I think he was proud that Tommy followed his heart for the career path he chose to follow. Tommy also took a position with a local church. He would try his sermons out on me. Sometimes the whole family, including Judy, would be test subjects to Tommy's sermons. We would clap, say amens, and shout hallelujahs. Tommy would get so passionate that his passion would rub off on us, too.

ADOPTED

Tommy had met Judy, the love of his life, in high school. They would never part. I on the other hand, met the love of my life in university. When I first saw her in the library, I was instantly attracted to this beautiful, mysterious woman. She is about six feet tall, so she stood out from the crowd. Her hair was cut short and with a naturally tight curl, it looked like a curly halo. Her skin stood out from all of the people that surrounded her--in a sea of lighter skinned folk, her skin was like a medium-roasted coffee bean. Her skin was smooth and soft looking with a healthy sheen. Her body was well defined. She was as muscular as a young woman could be and still be captivatingly feminine. My mind was racing with ideas flashing like paparazzi camera flashes at a red-carpet event. How in the world was I going to meet this beautiful young lady.

God had read my wish-list. Of course, my insecure-self crashed its way into my thoughts. "She's way out of your league, shrub." But, on the other shoulder, my confident-self countered, "Just stroll over there and flash that Rashawn smile. She'll melt like butter for you, son." Unfortunately, that day my insecure-self won. Instead of approaching her, I grabbed the book I was interested in reading and sat at a different table. But I strategically sat at a table positioned in such a way that I could glance over my book to occasionally let my eyes drink in her beauty.

I was cool with all the guys, jocks and nerds. I was even cool around the girls at school, but this was my first real attraction. The sheer level of attraction intimidated me. I think my mom was worried when I didn't meet a girl that interested me at school. But it seems that dad was right and God had a plan all along.

As attracted and totally interested as I was in this girl, I was a total rookie at putting any plan or strategy together for an approach. I just sat there with the book in my hands, but I couldn't concentrate on my work. I couldn't even focus on the words I was trying to read. Meanwhile, my emotions were so confused that my head was swirling. On the one hand, I was so excited that my eyes had seen this beautiful woman. On the other hand, I was uncomfortable feeling so vulnerable that I couldn't talk to her. I'm not a kid, I thought to myself! My thoughts were swimming around in my head so much that I didn't even notice that she had moved from where she was sitting and sat right in front of me. When I did notice, I had an involuntary reflex that wasn't my best cool self.

"Oh-shoot! You're here! I mean, hi there. No, no, no, please let me start over. Hello, my name is Rashawn, Rashawn Wright."

She giggled and replied teasingly, "Hi, Rashawn, Rashawn Wright. My name is, Hailey Carmen Diaz. I don't want you to think that I'm forward or anything but I saw you watching me while you were trying to read. Are reading 'Law School Confidential'? I'm curious, what do you think of Miller's approach to equipping first year students to navigate the complexities of L-1?"

Dang! She hit me with a good question right off the bat, but I smiled a smile of relief, thinking, "She's talking my language--not only is she beautiful but she's super intelligent and confident." I must have been relishing the moment too long because I was interrupted.

"Well sir, do you have an opinion on the book that you're reading or not?"

I mentally scolded myself for talking to myself instead of her. "Come on you, fool, don't mess this up!" Then I calmly answered, "I highly recommend this book for any first-year law student. No offense, but aren't you a little young for a first-year law student?"

She made that sweet, giggling sound again, "No offense taken, but aren't you a little young for a first-year law student, too?"

I looked into those brown eyes and said, "Oh, I see what you did there."

We both laughed so loud that the librarian, an older lady in classic librarian glasses gave us a look and a shush.

I lowered my voice and quietly asked, "You want to go somewhere we can talk?"

Hailey looked me full in the eyes, "Yeah, I think I'd like that."

We took our time as we walked to the coffee shop, chatting as we strolled through the campus. It was like we were best friends even though we had just met.

I sat across from Hailey, and she asked me, "So, what do you plan to do with your law degree?"

"Well, my dad has a law firm and it's always been his dream that his kids would work with him. It's my dream as well, and so far, I'll probably will be the first of us kids to work at the firm."

"How many children are in your family?"

"There's four of us in total; two of us are adopted. My older brother and sister have already passed the bar. Both of them are working in Virginia at the orphanage where my dad and mom found Tommy and myself. It's called the Wright Farm.

Hailey's eyes widened, "Wait a minute, and that's your name! You mean to tell me that your family owns an orphanage? That's so cool."

"Well, that's a long story, but yeah, kinda-sorta."

As I looked into her dark brown eyes, they seemed to match the color of her skin perfectly. Her full lips seemed to pout even when she smiled. Her lips looked like they were offering me a warm, refreshing drink, and it was all I could do to not think about kissing Hailey.

Suddenly I heard, "Earth to Rashawn! Where did you go just now?"

I didn't want to sound corny and say, "I just went into your eyes." So instead, I said, "Oh, I'm sorry, I was just thinking of something."

She smiled that lovely smile, and with a twinkle in her eye, it was almost as if she had read my thoughts. She slyly said, "Or maybe, thinking about someone? Let's get back to work, Mr. Rashawn, and you can think about whatever that was you were thinking, later."

As we hurried back to the library, our stride was at a quicker pace than before. Our arms were swinging, and our hands slightly brushed together. This time both of us giggled, and in the rhythm of the return swing, I took a chance. Opening my hand, I caught her hand. It was a big risk, but it paid off. Hailey looked away, but I could tell that she was smiling. We held hands, swinging them to the rhythm of our stride. Then, she flashed a smile directly at me as if to give me the ok to walk a little bit closer. Don't ask me how or why, but more than walking closer, I think our souls connected that very first day. From then on, I thought about Hailey just about every day. We called and texted each other daily. We were best friends long before anything else. There was nothing I couldn't talk to Hailey about. Just as dad had said, I had found my best friend and we were falling in love together.

CHARLES LEE KNUCKLES

Love Would Face Tests That Only Made Love Stronger

One day, things suddenly changed and Hailey started acting strange. The prior few months, we had been spending all of our time together, but now she was avoiding me on campus. It was hard to run into her off campus as well, and when I did, she would brush me off with lame excuses. I knew we were coming up on final exams, so I thought maybe the pressure was getting to her. Finals strike fear in the hearts of many students. But it made no sense that Hailey would be fearful. My girl is smart and she lived for academic challenges. So, I was confused about why her behavior had changed so suddenly.

Finally, one day in the library, I cornered Hailey.

I asked, "Hey, what's going on? You know that you can talk to me. Let me in!"

ADOPTED

She looked at me when the librarian, as usual, shushed us. As I thought to myself, "If that silly librarian only knew how important this is, she wouldn't shush us."

At that moment, tears started falling from Hailey's eyes. She mumbled through her tears, "Rashawn, I can't get you involved! I will not be the reason that you get hurt!"

Then, Hailey ran out of the library, leaving me baffled. But it was too late, she was the woman that I love. If she was hurting, I wanted to be the one to rescue her! I ran after her, leaving our books and backpacks. I've got to tell you, that girl is fast. It seemed that she was already halfway across the campus, but I pursued her, running as fast as I could. Ignoring the "Keep off Grass" sign, I ran across the manicured lawn to cut her off. Hailey was still frantic, but I stepped in front of her and stopped her by wrapping my arms around her and lifting her off the ground.

In the air, her legs were still running as she shouted in my face, "LET ME GO, RASHAWN!"

I kissed her on her tears and gently replied, "I will never let you go. I'll always be here for you. I will always love you. Hailey Carmen Diaz. I'm not letting you go, so let me in. You are not alone in whatever this is, Hailey."

She finally surrendered, her legs stopped moving, her body went limp, and she sank into my arms. Now, with her feet on the ground and her arms around my waist, Hailey's head rested on my chest, and I could feel her deep sobs as they went into my chest.

She caught her breath and said, "Rashawn, what am I going to do? I'm trapped."

I took her face in my hands, "First, tell me everything that's going on and then, we'll figure out what **we** are going to do about it."

"Two men are trying to force me to do what I don't want to do. They are both powerful men in different ways. One is Professor Joyner. He's pressuring me about my midterm exam in his class. I know I can pass it easily, but he is implying that I will only pass his test if he gets what he wants. He wants me to have sex with him."

Immediately, anger flared up inside of me, but my dad had taught me the value of remaining calm during high pressure situations. I replied, "Sounds like our Criminal Law professor is himself a criminal. Let me ask you something Hailey, are you ok with us taking this to my dad?"

"No, Rashawn. It's hard enough talking to you about this."

"Yeah, I know, but we need my dad in on this one. Trust me Hailey, he can come up with an effective plan. I've seen him handle this sort of thing before. Don't worry, my mom will sit in and help you feel more comfortable."

"Rashawn, I haven't told you everything yet. There's another guy stalking me. His name is Jarrad. He's from the neighborhood and he's known me for years."

"Hailey, how long did you date this guy?"

"Actually, I've never dated him. However, I was courteous to him. I spoke to him when he spoke to me in the neighborhood. We've only had a few conversations. That's the extent of our relationship but he wants something more. I think everyone thinks just because I'm tall that I've had sex, but I haven't. He wants to be romantic with me but I put him

ADOPTED

off by telling him that I was saving myself for my marriage. I made it very clear to Jarrad that I was not interested, but he doesn't seem to hear me. He knows my routine, my travel route, and almost daily, he's intercepting me and putting a lot of pressure on me. Jarrad is saying that he's waited long enough and because I live in his hood, that I belong to him. He's scary dangerous, Rashawn. You can see why I don't want you to get involved, can't you? I don't want you to get hurt because of me!"

Hailey was crying uncontrollably, and I knew what to do, for now. I just held her in my arms, and as I rocked her back and forth, I kept saying, "I've got you, trust me, I've got you, Hailey Carmen Diaz".

For now, we were at peace as time seemed to slow down in our deep embrace.

My dad would know exactly what to do about the professor and I, on the other hand, knew exactly how to handle Hailey's stalker, this Jarrad character. I knew many Jarrads back in the old neighborhood. I'd watched them intimidate girls back then and I always wanted to shut them down. Now it was personal!

Hailey and I walked to the ice cream parlor off-campus. We sat outside and enjoyed the warm summer's day with our favorite ice cream cones. I think the thing we liked about ice cream cones is that you have to lick them with the focus of keeping the melting ice cream from running down the cone onto your hand. It always made us giggle. With the ice cream cones fending off our worries, we were able to look into each other's eyes the way we loved to do whenever we were together. Our eyes danced like they do when they connect, and our troubles, at least for a time, seemed far away. We even breathed differently. Our friendship was stronger than any obstacle. I knew that I didn't want Hailey to feel any pressure about sex from me. I just wanted our friendship to thrive. It was sweeter than any of the fifty flavors of ice cream at the creamery.

Later, at home, as Hailey sat with me and mom, waiting for dad in the den where he relaxed and read his newspaper. Mom was so happy that I had finally found a girl to whom I was attracted. She was eager to befriend Hailey. Mom was trying to nail down a date when they could have a girl's spa day when dad walked in the room. Dad was smart enough that he didn't interrupt mom's mission, so he let mom finish what she was trying to do before interrupting.

Then, he gently cleared his throat and asked, "What's going on?" Is there a family meeting I wasn't informed about? Anybody going to introduce me to our lovely guest?"

Our family dynamic seemed to put Hailey at ease, but even so, she turned to me and without words and with only her eyes, she asked me to lead.

I just came right out with it, "Dad, meet my friend Hailey. Hailey and I are here because her law professor, Professor Joyner, is making inappropriate advances to her at university. He's pressuring her!"

Mom was also hearing this for the first time, so she scooted closer to Hailey and hugged her. Turning to dad, mom said, "David, I don't care what you're doing. You've got to take her case."

Hailey was sobbing on mom's shoulder. The hug comforted Hailey.

Dad said to mom, "Susan, let's get the facts first. You and Rashawn let the girl talk."

Mom loosened her hug, and started rubbing Hailey's shoulders as she spoke between sobs, "Mr. Wright, I'm a good student. I know criminal law well, but the professor is so critical of my work, it's intimidating. My mom cannot afford to pay for my education. The professor knows that my scholarship depends on my grades. He knows that I can't afford for my grades to drop. He's got the upper hand. Mr. Wright, without my scholarship, I'm out of law school. He makes me stay after class and whenever he gets me alone, he keeps suggesting that he can make things go smoothly for me if I cooperate with him."

Any kind of injustice infuriates my dad, and it was clear that, after hearing Hailey's story, he was very angry. "Hailey, my wife, Susan, is right! Don't worry about a fee, you won't owe anything. I have to do everything in my power to make this right. First, we must gather evidence. Don't let the professor see you do this, but I want you to document every encounter you have with him, thoroughly. Dates, times, locations, events and any potential witnesses. To an extent, you're going to have to endure some of his behaviors in order to bring him to justice."

Then dad turned to me, "Son, I can see that you care deeply for Hailey, but you're going to have to keep your head through all of this. Whatever you do, you do not confront this creep! If we could only get some of this on video…"

When dad said video, I smiled because I knew exactly who to ask for help. "Leave that to me dad, I'll get my big bro', Tommy, to help."

Hailey didn't have to do anything different. She just went about her day as usual. She studied hard and turned in her assignments. She secretly hoped that the professor would forget about her and things would go back to normal. But the professor was fixated on Hailey's tall, lean, and muscular body. It certainly was through no fault of her own and had nothing to do with anything that she was doing. He was like a moth drawn to a flame, and he was about to get burnt!

In the meantime, dad had a confidential conversation with the Dean, and he secured written permission for Tommy to place surveillance cameras. I need not remind anyone that my big bro', Tommy, is a genius; he was able to secretly plant several cameras.

True to form, it did not take long for the professor to make his move. He singled Hailey out. "Hailey, let's take a look at your paper on 'The Rationales for Allowing Discretion, and the Proper Scope of Discretion.'"

Hailey's work was perfect. For added evidence, Dad had checked it and said that it was a brilliant paper. Hailey covered topics like, 'The Fourth Amendment and Police Discretion', and 'Why is Discretion Important in Police Work'. She even created a 'Cost-Benefit Analysis of Police Discretion'.

Even though dad had said that her work was exceptional, the professor called Hailey on the side and proceeded to poke holes in her work. With critique after critique, he pummeled her with discouragement and despair. It was clear that this was a malicious use of his authority. The cameras caught everything. Professor Joyner was building the case against himself.

Then, in front of all the other students and in front of the camera, he told her that if she ever expected a passing grade, she would have to come back at the end of the day.

After class, we all held a secret meeting in the room with all the video viewing equipment. Some of the equipment was supplied by the Dean, but my big bro', Tommy, had the fancy stuff. We all waited in the room, peering at the monitors--Tommy, dad, Dean Jacobs, a police detective and myself. Dad and Detective Reynolds had a plan for Hailey's strategy, but Hailey stopped them.

"Gentlemen, I'm not going to do anything deceptive or be suggestive. I'm going to present my paper, but I will not give him any indication that what he is doing is acceptable. I'm not going to set him up. As a matter of fact, I'm praying that he is discouraged in his attempts to manipulate me."

I was so proud of Hailey.

The detective said, "OK, let's get you down there and see what happens. Do we need to get her fitted for a wire?"

Tommy said proudly, "No need for a wire, I've got the room set for video and audio. If he whispers, we'll hear him, and most importantly, we'll see him."

Dad added, "If things get crazy and he goes too far, we've got to get in there fast! And remember Rashawn, keep your hands off of him. Let the law do its work. Let Detective Reynold do any restraining necessary. OK, let's go, it's time."

The camera picked up as Hailey walked into the room. She asked, "Where's everyone else, Professor Joyner? Aren't you grading other papers?"

The professor moved to the door and locked it. "No, Hailey it's just you and me for today. You're going to have all of my attention." He smiled and said, "Together, we're going to get your work into shape so that you can get a passing grade and keep your scholarship. You do want to keep your scholarship, don't you?"

"But, Professor Joyner, in my opinion my paper is excellent work. I thoroughly researched my work and chose important information, fitting the perimeters of the assignment."

Watching from the next room, we all were concerned, but it was Detective Reynolds that cursed and said, "That girl is going to blow the case for us! This is going to be a complete waste of my time."

Nevertheless, the professor was not deterred. As I watched, I thought out loud, "He must have done this thing many times before."

Dad agreed, "Yes son, he's got this down pat. There have got to be other victims."

Then the professor, with his hand on Hailey's hip, moved her over to the podium. He then put her papers on the podium as if he was going to help her amend them. He made his move and slid in behind her to make body contact. Hailey froze in fear.

Detective Reynolds got excited, "That-a-girl! Let's see how far he's going to go!"

ADOPTED

All the while, Professor Joyner was psychologically attacking her confidence. Hailey was frozen like a gazelle in the jaws a lion. He started rubbing his hand up and down on her lower back. Occasionally, the professor would pull her close to his body. He kissed her on the neck.

I said to the detective, "Do we move in now?"

"Hold on, son, let's give him a little more rope."

Then, the professor slipped his hand under Hailey's top, and reflectively she turned around and punched him in the nose. The professor grabbed her hands and pinned her to the podium. His face was fixed with an evil grin as he said, "So you like it rough, huh?"

If the detective hadn't shouted, "Now! Move, move, move, quick, get him", I would have busted into the room.

Dean Jacobs quickly unlocked the door. Our noise startled the professor. I ran to Hailey and took her in my arms. The detective moved in on the professor and cuffed him.

The professor protested, "Why are you handcuffing me, I think she broke my nose. Arrest that little..."

The detective interrupted Professor Joyner, "You have the right to keep silent, anything thing you say can be used in a court of law. You have the right to an attorney, and if you can't afford one, one will be appointed to you. And you know what mister, I would exercise that right to keep silent, if I were you."

The detective marched the professor out of the university. He perp-walked him right in front of the faculty and students.

The students started laughing. "Hey Professor Joyner, what did you get caught doing? Want to share with the class, professor?"

But what was even more disturbing, the faculty seemed not to be surprised. We had stopped a monster. But dad and I knew he had not become a monster overnight. I was committed to corporate law, but this event fueled Hailey's desire to go into criminal law. Instead of becoming a defense attorney, she now decided to work for the District Attorney's office.

Later, we gave our statements at the police station for the detective. With Dean Jacobs' statement included, the case against Professor Joyner was rock solid. Dad had everything he needed for the civil case. He almost never took cases like this one. Dad would normally hand pro-bono cases to one of his junior associates. This case was different. He had walked it through this far and now, it was personal. Dad prepared Hailey's case and saw it all the way through. Not only would he sue the professor personally, but he would go on to sue the university as well. Hailey was well represented. Seeing Hailey's courage, just as dad and I had thought, other female students came forward.

As a result of the new victims, there was a media frenzy. In a news conference, Dean Jacobs said, "The university will do the right thing. We will cooperate with the justice system to the best of our ability. This situation with Professor Joyner is like a decayed tooth that must be extracted."

There is something about ice cream cones that centered Hailey and I. We would watch each other while eating the ice cream cones. Eating ice cream cones together would make us smile and laugh and forget about everything but that moment in time while licking our ice cream cones. There was a wonderful little creamery right around the corner from Hailey's home. It wasn't a chain, just a little mom and pop shop. We had our favorite flavors, mine was butter pecan and Hailey loved her strawberries and cream.

Usually, I would finish my cone first. I was just biting the bottom off of my cone when right in front of us appeared an intense looking young man. It turned out that this was the infamous Jarrad. I was meeting my evil nemesis for the first time. Jarrad blocked our way like in an old spaghetti western with the showdown between hero and villain. As we paused in midstride, I could almost hear the Spanish acoustical guitar and flute that accompanies the final showdown in old cowboy movies.

There we were, face to face. Hailey seemed to panic. As strong as Hailey is, Jarrad had a psychological advantage over her. Over time, being creepy, he had made her fearful of him. I, on the other hand, had known the Jarrads of the world most of my life. I wanted him to underestimate me. I acted a little corny, smiling, and saying something goofy like, "You must be Hailey's friend."

I stuck out my hand to shake his, while my purpose was to simply close the distance between us. I knew by his posture that Jarrad was armed. I said, "If I had known we were going to meet, I would have bought you an ice cream cone, too."

Jarrad grimaced and mean-mugged at me, just like the bad guy in an old-school cowboy movie would do. Then, in an attempt to intimidate me, he growled, "I don't want any stinking ice cream! Today, punk, you're going to learn to keep away for my female!"

I asked a silly question, "I had no idea that Hailey is your female. When did that happen?"

As harmless as I could, I took one more step forward. I was finally close enough. Jarrad seemed to sense something had changed in my demeanor and went for his gun. But I smothered him, and with my hand on his hand, I shoved it back into the waistline of the front of his pants. At the same time, all in one motion, I put my foot behind his foot, wrapping my free hand around his neck, I tripped him backwards to the ground. As we hit the ground, there was a thunderous roar! The gun had fired a shot. The three of us were frozen for a second.

Hailey screamed, "I knew this would happen!" She didn't know who was shot. She was crying hysterically as she shouted, "I'm so sorry, Rashawn, I didn't mean to get you hurt. I love you!"

Then, as I laid still on top of Jarrad, he let out a loud moan and began to sob. "I'm shot, help me!"

But I wasn't going to move yet. I kept my position, pinning him down with my body, and keeping my hand on his gun hand and my other elbow on his throat.. Then, I said in a calm voice, "Jarrad, you've got to release the gun before I can help you."

"How do I know that you won't shoot me again?"

Calmly, I said, "Jarrad, I didn't shoot you in the first place. You shot yourself. I would never just shoot a person. I help people. I don't know what you were thinking, carrying a gun

ADOPTED

in your waistline in front of your pants. Let go of the gun, Jarrad. I want to make sure that we all are safe before I help you. You could be bleeding to death as we speak. If that bullet hit your femoral artery, you could be bleeding to death as we speak."

Hearing the possibility that he could bleed to death, Jarrad finally let go of the gun. I took it, but I kept him pinned, as I immediately took the clip out and ejected the last bullet from the chamber. Jarrad had shot through his right testicle, and the bullet traveled down his leg, crashing into his left kneecap. Hailey had already called the police and ambulance.

I told Jarrad, "We have to put pressure on where you're hit. You're going have to put pressure on your privates, while I take care of your knee."

Jarrad was very fortunate that he did not hit his femoral artery. I took off my shirt and used it to tie around his knee.

Jarrad then said, "Hey, man, thanks for helping me." Then he said, "My [n-word], would you get rid of the gun, so I don't catch a gun charge?"

As disgusted as I was with Jarrad, I still didn't want him to die. But as far as covering up his crime, that was out of the question. "Don't use the n-word with me, Jarrad, and no, I can't do that. The law is very clear in this situation. Besides, you intended to shoot me with that gun. We're going to tell the truth about what you tried to do, Jarrad. They will probably charge you for attempted murder. Maybe you can do something productive in prison, like find God and go to school. I'd be happy to come visit you and help you plan a new life. I'll help you as much as I can, but only within the law."

Jarrad just laid his head back and relaxed a little. As we all waited for the ambulance and police, Jarrad said, "Look man, I wasn't really going to shoot you. I was just trying to intimidate you so I could try to get with Hailey. But I can see your point. I guess it's not cool, threatening people with guns. You sure you can't give me a break, and get rid of the gun?"

"No man, I'm not doing that. How many crimes have you committed with that gun?"

At that point, Jarrad just lowered his head. He looked like he had just surrendered to reality.

We could hear sirens in the distance heading towards us. They were getting closer and closer. I could feel Hailey's eyes on me, so I turned and smiled at her. She didn't need me to say anything. It's funny how love can flow from one person to another without even a word or a touch. The power of eye contact is amazing. Right then, I knew that Hailey knew that with me she was safe. Later that day, she would tell me that she knew that I was the man that God created for her, that she knew that I would love her and protect her. I was her rescuer.

I took her hands and looked into her eyes and said, "And you rescued me as well."

I went to visit Jarrad in the hospital, right before he was sent to jail. I felt sorry for him. I went there to tell him about God.

"Hey, Jarrad, how are you feeling, brother?"

Jarrad sat up in bed, his wrist handcuffed to the bed. "How do you think I feel? Look man, I want to apologize to you. I only brought the gun to intimidate you and Hailey. Things got way out of hand."

"Jarrad, I'm not here to talk about that. I realize that you may have just wanted to intimidate us but to what end? Hailey could never love you. You made her fear you."

Jarrad looked down, as he continued to speak, "Look man, my mom and dad abandoned me to the streets. I don't know any other way."

"Look at me Jarrad." I looked him in the eyes and said, "My mom was killed because of her addiction to heroin. I don't even know what my dad looks like. There's no difference between you and me--we came up the same way."

Jarrad looked at me intensely, "Why you lying, man? You've got parents."

"Jarrad, I grew up in the streets until my early teens. Then, I was adopted twice. First, as a young teen, I was adopted by God, then, I was adopted by my parents. Jarrad, it's never too late. You can be adopted by God, right now, today."

Jarrad let me pray for him and accepted Christ as his Lord and Savior.

"Jarrad, when you get to prison, connect with some Christians and get into a Christian ministry. There will be chaplains. Find a Christian Chaplain and connect with Bible studies. I'm going to send you a Bible and the first story I want you to read is the story of Joseph in the book of Genesis. In the story, Joseph goes to prison, just like you. What makes Joseph's story important to you is that you will see, because of Joseph's love for God, everyone else in the prison was in prison, but not Joseph--he was in an opportunity. Jarrad, you can either be in prison or you can be in an opportunity. That choice is yours. Find all of the educational opportunities you can and love the Lord with all of your heart, mind, soul and strength, and let Him shape you into the man He designed you to be."

I visited Jarrad a couple more times. It turns out that he took my advice.

Hailey and I recovered after the ambush drama with Jarrad. Soon, we both were back, fully focused on the process of pursuing our Juris Doctor Degree before we would take the bar. We were so in love that we decided we had to get married. Hailey's mom and dad and my mom and dad got together and half-heartly tried to talk us into finishing our education and passing the bar before we got married. They made a lot of sense but we just couldn't wait. We wanted to be and do everything together from then on, as man and wife.

We were planning a small wedding in Brooklyn. But then my brother, Jeff, my sister, Rennie, my brother-in-law, Will, and the whole family, found out. They all insisted that the wedding be held in Virginia in the chapel on the Wright Farm Orphanage for Boys, where it all began. Hailey and I agreed. We decided that it made perfect sense for us all to meet in Virginia for the wedding.

While still in Brooklyn, mom and dad, Tommy and Judy, Hailey and I, were all having dinner, when my brother, Tommy, started secretly motioning me to come with him to the den. I didn't know what to expect. Tommy had a strange gleam in his eyes as he said, "Lil' bro', I don't want to be intrusive or

ADOPTED

rain on your parade or anything like that, but Judy and I want to get married, too. Would you be opposed to making it a double wedding?"

Immediately, I had tears in my eyes, "Big bro', I don't know why you don't already know? Tommy, that would make me so happy. Do you realize how epic that would be? We're going back home so different from when we left and we are bringing joy!"

When we returned to the table where everyone was still talking, I was trying to keep my cool, but Tommy blurted it out, "Guess what, everybody. Judy and I are getting married, too. We're having a double wedding!"

Oh, my, the family went into a frenzied chatter. It seemed like all the women were able to talk at the same time. Dad just sat there looking at us and smiling, like he was having his best day ever. It was decided, and the women were already in the planning stage. We would return to the Farm. For some reason, we all decided to drive instead of flying.

We were happy that we drove instead of flying--it was so much more intimate. The drive was only about seven hours. The six of us fitted in dad's SUV, comfortably. We chatted and laughed almost the whole way.

At the Farm, Tommy and I sat with young boys. As I looked across that sea of fresh faces, I could almost see the young Tommy and me in the crowd. It took us back, and later that night, we shared our testimonies with the guys. Hailey and Judy, our wives-to-be, both looked on in wonderment as we unfolded the stories of our miraculous journeys from death to life.

CHARLES LEE KNUCKLES

It was all so cool that Mr. Thomas came out to see us. As I recounted the story of how I got to the Farm, I could see the look on Mr. Thomas' face. Both Tommy and I spoke of our life-changing encounters with Mr. Thomas. He seemed to be in tears as the accounts emotionally touched him. We didn't know whether he had known that he meant so much to us. Both Tommy and I confessed that, as young men, we were in search of real masculine role models, solid men, and we had found none in the old neighborhoods. Both of our birth fathers had failed us. Teachers in the old neighborhood were so fearful of either confrontations or making mistakes, that it seemed to us as though they were too distant to care, and that our lives didn't matter to them. All but a few were like jelly, more fearful of their jobs than they were committed to making a difference. However, in our short time with him, Mr. Thomas demonstrated real masculinity. He was strong when he broke up that fight when I was just about to get stomped. But he was gentle when he knew I was ready to throw in the towel and give up. He was not afraid to be funny, but it was with a clean humor, and higher standard of funny than we were used to hearing. And Mr. Thomas was not ashamed of his faith in Christ. For Tommy and me, he was the first solid masculine role model we had known. Then, there was Mr. Will, and ultimately our dad, David Wright.

Tommy and I got in such a rhythm, talking about the Farm, that we started talking in unison and finishing each other's sentences, again. That's when Will jumped up and shouted, "You guys still do that? You still both talk at the same time! How in the world do you do that?"

ADOPTED

Tommy and I looked at each other and busted out laughing. We retold the snitching story, just as we originally had told it to Will. We used to call him Mr. Will but now that he's our brother in-law, he's just Will to us...unless we're in front of the boys of the Farm or the girls at the plantation, then it's Mr. Will.

After the talk, we all just milled around. Our fiancées hung out together with our sister Rennie as Tommy and I socialized with the boys. One boy kept following me around until he got a chance to talk to me.

I asked, "What's your name young man?"

He answered, "I am Eugene Chen Trinh, but my friends call me Geno. My family is from Vietnam, but they are no longer alive."

I said, "Geno, I'm very sorry for your loss. Do you have any relatives?"

"No, Mr. Rashawn, we were very poor. Where we lived was dangerous, and now, as far as I know, they are all dead. They died in a house fire. It's still a mystery how that fire started. I was the only one who survived because I was outside."

His story reminded me of my brother Tommy's story.

Geno continued, "I was picked up running the streets and getting into trouble. At the time, I was ten years old. I'm thirteen, now. I met Mr. Thomas and Mr. Will and I have heard stories about you and your brother. I wanted to meet you."

Geno and I talked and spent the rest of the day together. Everyone seemed to be able to see our bond and gave us space. This kid had seen so much pain and hurt and yet he was intelligent and well-mannered. It was then that I was beginning to realize what dad felt when he met Tommy and me. I decided that I would mentor Geno, maybe even adopt him.

The next day, Tommy, dad, Will, I, and our brother Jeff, who was now vice president of the Farm, all hung out. I asked Will if Geno could join us. Will gave Geno permission to do his chores later so he could spend more time with me.

Rennie, on the other hand, took all the women including my mom and Will's mom over to the girl's orphanage, the old Wright Plantation. Hailey and Judy would, later that night, tell Tommy and me how they were amazed by the plantation. They decided right away to plan for future visits. They made real connections to some girls and they wanted to stay in touch and perhaps mentor them.

It was two days before the wedding. Will, his parents, and Jeff had everything ready for the big day. The double wedding was happening!

ADOPTED

The Wedding: Told by Tommy Wright

The whole Jamison family were already at the chapel. I could not believe it. I hadn't seen Will's mom and dad, Jim and Emma Jamison, in what seemed like ages. Will's sister, Grace, and his brother, Jim Jr., were already seated near the front on the groom's family side. Judy and Hailey's families had already come from New York, and they nearly filled the bride's family side. Dad was best man for both Rashawn and I. Jeff was one of groomsmen along with two of our friends from New York, and then, there was Rashawn's last-minute groomsman, Eugene Chen Trinh, his new friend from the Farm. Both Judy and Hailey's bridesmaids were all New Yorkers from family and school. It was a huge wedding party and, at the front, our wedding officiator was none other than Will Jamison. Rashawn and I stood at the end of the aisle, nervously shifting our weight from one side to the other. Dad winked at us and nodded his head in reassurance.

Then, suddenly there was the start of the bridal music.

Two of the most beautiful women in the world began their walk down the aisle. Mom and dad had picked the song by Patti Labelle & The Bluebells called "Down the Aisle." Nobody but the old folks had ever heard this song before, but even to us young people, it seemed perfectly appropriate.

Judy and Hailey, walking with their fathers, stepped slowly to the beat of the song. It seemed like time slowed down just for us to enjoy and savor every second of their beauty. Before the ladies got to the wedding arch, Will motioned me to one side of himself and Rashawn to the other. Our ladies walked to our sides, Judy to me, and Hailey to Rashawn.

Will opened his arms to point to two stands with boards on them. On each board was the scripture, "A cord of three strands is not easily broken." One board had our names inscribed, "Thomas and Judith", the other, "Rashawn and Hailey". At the bottom of the boards were three cords, two of the cords were golden and one blood red. As Will read from Ecclesiastes 4: 9-12, we were instructed that each couple together would braid their strands into one cord.

"Two are better than one, because they have a good return for their labor: If either of them falls down one can help the other up But pity anyone who falls and has no one to help them up. Also, if two lie down together, they will keep warm. But how can one keep warm alone? Though one may be overpowered, two can defend themselves. A cord of three strands is not quickly broken."

Judy and I braided our cords and so did Rashawn and Hailey. We had practiced so that we finished as Will finished the scripture. When we completed our cords of three strands, Will asked us to put our rings on each other as we said our personal vows.

Next, Will read Jesus' words from Mark 10, *"And Jesus answered and said to them, 'Because of the hardness of your heart, he wrote you this precept. But from the beginning of the creation, God made them male and female. For this reason, a man shall leave his father and mother and be joined to his wife, and the two shall become one flesh; so then they are no longer two, but one flesh. Therefore, what God has joined together, let not man separate.'"*

"I now pronounce you, "man and wife", and I now pronounce **you**, "man and wife". You both may kiss your brides. Ladies and gentlemen, I present to you, Mrs. and Mr. Thomas and Judith Wright, and I also present to you, Mr. and Mrs. Rashawn and Hailey Wright."

The crowd stood up as Rashawn and I tried to see who could kiss their wife the longest. We both won. We stopped our kisses at the same time, turned to the crowd, and they went wild. All of the people thunderously applauded, and there were whistles and shouts.

After the photographer finished the wedding photos, we partied all night at the reception. We danced, talked and laughed, almost until almost dawn.

In the morning, Hailey and Rashawn, Judy and I, boarded our flights and headed to the Florida Keys. We had beautiful suites in our hotel, but most of the time, we stayed on the water in a yacht. If not on the yacht, we were either in the ocean or the pool, swimming almost the whole time. Rarely were we dressed in anything but swimsuits. We must have used a gallon of sunscreen. We joked about the fact that we found spots to lounge where Judy and I were in the sun while Rashawn and Hailey were right next to us in the shade. We laughed about that so much.

On every reservation, there were the names, Wright and Wright. People had questions in their eyes but very few had the courage to ask. We were more than happy to explain that we were brothers. Then, all four of us would sit back and watch the reactions. It never got old.

Then came the sad moment that the honeymoons were over. That last day I had a confession to make to my brother. "Lil' bro', Judy and I aren't coming back to New York."

"What in the world are you talking about, Tommy?"

I could see the hurt and concern in Rashawn's eyes.

"We're going to stay in Virginia. I'm going to pastor a church in town. I applied and was accepted for lead pastor for Mount Carmel Church. I bought a house. Judy and I are going from here to our new home. My stuff was moved out of dad's house while we were here. I didn't have much to move. We have to buy furniture, but Virginia is going to be home for us now."

For the first time that I could ever remember, Rashawn was speechless. I looked into his eyes and said "Lil' bro', I've got a little wedding present for you and Hailey. I know that you were looking at an apartment in Brooklyn near mom and dad. I also know they want you two to move in with them, but here take these."

I took Rashawn's hand and put some keys in it. He looked at me with a confused look in his eyes. "Tommy, what are these?"

"Lil' bro', they are the keys to your new house. It's fully paid for. The deed is in your name and it's on your and Hailey's bed in the master suite. It's almost completely furnished, and it's close to mom and dad in Brooklyn."

Rashawn had tears in his eyes, "But bro', I can't accept a gift this big."

I smiled, "If you can't accept this from your brother, then who can you accept it from? Rashawn, you know I've been clever in my investments and I've got millions. I give stuff to all kinds of people. Let me give this to my brother. Don't turn me down, lil' bro, I love you more than this little gift can express. I've got to do this!"

Rashawn's face broke into a cry, "Dang, big bro', you done gone and made me cry an ugly cry in front of everybody."

Hailey leaned in and hugged Rashawn. She kissed one of his tears, and at that, we all started to cry and hug each other. Judy and Hailey, me and Rashawn, sobbing tears of joy.

"You won't miss me, lil' bro'. We are just a short, Highway 13, drive away. You can come and stay with us in Virginia and we can visit and stay with you in New York. It'll be fun!"

Our return flights were separate. Rashawn and Hailey went on to their new home in New York, first. I imagined them designing their new home to their taste. Me and Judy had put some fancy beds and kitchen appliances in it for them.

    Judy and I stayed on the water for two more days. We had waited a long time to be this intimate. I'm pretty sure that was when our oldest daughter was conceived. We named her after my mom, Susan Christina Wright.

ADOPTED

Adoption: Rashawn and Hailey

Ephesians 1:5
Having predestinated us unto the adoption of children by Jesus Christ to Himself, according to the good pleasure of His will,

Hailey and I loved our new home. In typical Tommy fashion, my big bro's generosity was extravagant. Our home was huge.

    The house was so big and I had come to love Geno so much, that one night I asked Hailey if could we adopt him. I thought it would take some convincing for Hailey to be onboard with the adoption. I was surprised how excited she was at the idea. We did most of the arrangements with my brother, Jeff, and Geno over the phone.

    Then came the day for us to ride down to the Farm to pick Geno up. We decided that, after the paperwork was all finished, we would enjoy some time on the Farm with our family and our new son. Hailey, Geno and I went horseback-riding along the old trail to the river. We went fishing and caught a healthy bunch of fish. After the ride back, we took care of the horses and retreated to one of the guest family cabins. We cooked our fish and sat around talking. Geno was right at home with us.

Early the next morning, we started our journey home. As Geno sat in the back seat, driving away from the Farm, I remembered the ride with Tommy, mom, dad and I. I didn't have to imagine what it must be like for Gino. I knew first-hand. Gino was our only child, but at least I had had Tommy with me. I glanced back through the rearview mirror and Geno was looking out the back window at the Farm, just like Tommy and I did as we rode away to our new home.

I thought I would use some of Mr. Thomas' games. "OK guys, this is not going to be a boring ride. First game we're going to play is 21 Questions. Here are the rules: Every one hundred miles, we each get to ask anybody in the car seven questions, and no short answers, please. It's a little over three hundred miles to home, so choose your questions and your targets well. We each get seven questions, but you can ask anyone anything. Because there's three of us, that's 21 questions all together in 300 miles. I'll go first and this counts as two questions; Who's hungry, first question, and the second is, what kind of food are you hungry for, Geno?"

Hailey was the first to say, "That's cheating, Rashawn."

We all laughed. Geno decided that he wanted a cheeseburger, fries and a shake. The ride went well and we talked all the way home. I loved the fact that Geno had no problem talking to Hailey and me.

We stood in front of the beautiful house that Tommy had bought for us. We let Geno take it all in.

Then, Geno asked, "I get to live here?"

Hailey answered, "I was thinking the same thing, Geno. Do we get to live here?"

Yes, we do, son., This is our home." I said, "Let's get inside with all this luggage."

We explored the house that was now our home. We let Geno pick which of the spare bedrooms he wanted. The house was fully furnished and my brother Tommy's choices had met Hailey's approval. She did make some small changes, but all in all, Tommy had good taste.

There was a family area in the basement that had video games, a big screen TV for movies and another one for the video games. My favorite is the workout area. It's equipped with an elliptical machine, a stationary bike and a multifunction, full body, weight-system machine. Geno's eyes lit up. Being a karate and wrestling champion, he loves to keep in shape.

I said, "Geno, we can jog around the neighborhood and the park if you can keep up."

He looked at me and smiled, "Can we go, now? I want to see if I can keep up."

We both laughed. We had on our sweats and sneakers, so we didn't even unpack, we headed out the door towards the park.

CHARLES LEE KNUCKLES

I said laughingly, "You have to follow, because you don't know where you're going yet!"

Geno laughed, and side by side, he matched me, step by step. I was loving our father-son relationship already. We had a long run and soon, it was getting dark. I showed Geno as many sights as I could for the first day.

When we got back, Hailey had ordered sandwiches and lemonade from the local deli for us. She said, "Next time we all jog together. Do you boys think you can keep up with a real track star?"

Geno said it so naturally, "I don't know, mom. We'll see."

Hailey laughed with delight. Geno had called her "mom." We sat in the great room talking and laughing until it was time to sleep. We all went to our rooms. I showered and then went to see how he was settling in. When I got to Geno's room, his door was slightly ajar, so, I peeped in and there was Geno on his knees praying. I looked for a moment and went back to Hailey. Then we prayed, thanking God for how He loves us so well.

It turns out that Geno did not know his parents. He was much too young when he was given to the Vietnamese family who told him his story. Geno said, "All I can remember is what my foster parents told me. They said that they had brought me to America from Vietnam. Besides running the streets of Richmond from the age of five, I don't remember much about coming to America. From how I lived, I'm just lucky to be alive. However, I am rather large for a Vietnamese. At least, I was the largest in my family of kids. As I look back, there were a lot of us, and I don't think any of us kids were related to the couple who kept us."

Geno fell in love with New York. He was fascinated by the sheer volume of everything. He did amazingly well in school. Just like my brother, Tommy, Geno is a mathlete and an athlete, as well. Besides his scholastic achievements, Geno also excelled in gymnastics, wrestling and karate. Geno not only did well in all of his classes, he was also very social. He was a confident kid, and he fit right in with the kids at school. Hailey and I did everything we could to cultivate his confidence, generosity, and concern for others. We were blessed. Geno was so easy to parent that he made us look good.

There came a time when I wanted Geno to enjoy the Vietnamese culture. So, one day, I took Geno to meet some Vietnamese friends. I took him to an area where Hailey and I sometimes shopped. We were friendly with a family that owned a restaurant. We would eat at their restaurant and sometimes at their home. I introduced Geno to my friend, Tim Tran, who I had come to know over the years at church.

I made this introduction, "Tim, meet my son, Geno. He is Vietnamese, but he doesn't know much about his heritage. So, Tim, if it's alright with you, I thought maybe you could figure out something about him, region of origin or, I don't know, anything that would be helpful?"

I figured that I had made it awkward enough so I stopped talking.

Tim looked at Geno and then, he turned to me, "Rashawn, my friend. I can see how desperate you both are to know something about young Geno. The one thing I can tell you is that he is not Vietnamese. More than likely he is a Pacific Islander. From which island, I cannot tell you."

Geno and I turned to each other in surprise.

Geno asked Tim, "Sir, are you sure?"

"Yes, Geno I'm sorry but I'm pretty sure."

I could see the look in Geno's eyes. What he had thought about himself, his very origin, was not true. He was hurt. So, I did the only thing I could think of to do. I hugged him.

We thanked Tim and we promised to see him in church on Sunday. Then, we left to go to the one place that our family processes best, the creamery, for ice cream cones. With our favorite ice cream cones in hand (mine, butter pecan, his, chocolate), we found a bench. We didn't talk much then. We just enjoyed the time with each other and our delicious treats.

Finally, Geno looked at me somberly and said, "Dad, you do know that we're going to have to run a couple miles after eating these?"

We both laughed and dug in on our ice cream cones, smiling, and laughing. The worst of the bad news was over, or so we thought.

As we sat, an idea came to me and I blurted it out to Geno, "I know what we'll do! We'll get ancestry kits for the whole family! I'll do one, you can do one and maybe, if she wants to join us, Hailey will do one."

Geno looked at me with delight in his eyes and said, "That's a great idea dad!"

We finished our cones.

ADOPTED

He looked down the running path, then looked at me. "Dad, I feel like I don't have to know my ancestry. I am a member of the Wright family, and I'm blessed. I think that's all I need to know right now. By the way, think you can keep up dad?"

We laughed, and off we ran. We raced, at first. Then, we relaxed the pace. Then, side by side, we just enjoyed the run. From that day on, Geno called me "dad," and each time he said it, he made me happy.

We took the ancestry test and weeks later the tests came back. My ancestry was from Cameroon, Sierra Leone, Ireland, and Mexico. Hailey's ancestry was from Nigeria, Cameroon, and India. However, Geno was Polynesian with specific indications of a secluded island we had never heard of, called Vanuvia.

We were all happy to get our results, especially to bring Geno a little closer to his origins. We talked about a family trip to Vanuvia one year, maybe right before Geno went to college. Little did we know that our DNA search had triggered an alert to certain people in Vanuvia.

One day, two men approached Geno on his way home from school. One of the men approached Gino from behind and put his hand on Geno's shoulder, and said, "You must come with us."

Reaching behind, Geno flipped him to the ground.

With the man's arm in an armbar, Geno looked the other man firm in the eye and said, "Stay where you are or I'll break his arm."

CHARLES LEE KNUCKLES

All of us Wright boys were formidable in self-defense but Geno, at only 15 years old, was next-level.

The man on the ground looked up at Gino and said, "We mean you no harm. We want to show you where you come from, and who you are in the place where you were born. You come from royalty. You are a prince and you could be the next king of our home-- your home."

Geno let the man up and said, "I'm sorry, but you don't sneak up on people from behind in this city. I thought that you meant me harm."

The man bowed, and then said, "Harm you? Never! You are of royalty on our island."

That's when Geno called me at work. "Dad, some men just approached me coming home from school."

I interrupted, "I'm on my way and I'm calling the police."

"No police, dad, they say that they are from the island where I was born. Can you come and hear what they have to say please?"

"I'm already in my car, son. Take them to the house, but don't take them in until I get there." On the way, I thought about that darn ancestry test, and now, I might lose my son because of it.

The men were very courteous. Hailey, Geno and I listened closely to their story. Apparently, Geno's mother and father were king and queen of the island. Geno's mom was pregnant during a military coup. The military overthrew the monarchy, forcing Geno's mother and father to flee to Vietnam. Then, Geno was born in Hanoi, Vietnam. Geno's parents were hunted relentlessly. Unfortunately, it wasn't long before

ADOPTED

Geno's parents were killed by a paid assassin. Right before the assassin struck, Geno's parents hid him at a street market right beside a Pho restaurant.

The kindly Vietnamese family found the baby in an alley and took Geno in as their own. However, this family was not without their own problems. The Trinh family came from a providence just south of Hanoi. They ran an honest business but when a local Hanoi drug lord tried to force them to use their Pho restaurant as a front to sell drugs and launder money, they refused. They went to the police and the police setup a sting operation that took the drug lord down. The gang vowed to kill the Trinh family, so they fled to the United States. They had also given evidence against the drug lord to the CIA.

When the young couple relocated to America, they gravitated to the Vietnamese community where part of the crime syndicate recognized them and ordered a hit on the family. The children were spared and that's how Geno ended up running the streets. No one from the island knew Geno existed, that is, until we did that darn ancestry test kit. Now, I was wondering if it had been worth it.

"Young Geno," said the man who seemed to be the spokesman, "Do you know your birthname?"

Geno replied, "Yes, I think I do, it's Eugene Trinh."

"No! Your birth name is Ariihau Haunui. Your first name means, 'King of Peace', and your last name means, 'The Great Peace'. So, you can see why many of your people think that your return to Vanuvia is prophetic, and that you will bring peace to us."

I was way out of my depth. I don't know why I interrupted but I did, "Geno, if you want to go see your homeland, we will go as a family."

Geno was in deep thought, and then he looked up at us all and said, "Look, I don't know about this prophecy stuff. I do know that I am a member of the Wright family. I know that I love the Lord Jesus. This is the only real family that I want to know. My life is good. I don't really want to go to any island or be anybody's king!"

I quickly intervened, "Alright gentlemen, you've got your answer. I'll see you to the door."

But Geno wasn't finished, "Dad, I think that I have to go. It will haunt me if I don't."

Hailey chimed in, "It's settled, let's pack our things, we're on our way to Vanuvia."

We started to call it, "Geno's Island."

We flew to L.A. and from L.A. to Ninoy Aquino International Airport, Manila. We landed and then took a smaller plane. Flying for hours, we finally landed on a fairly large island, with a sigh of relief. But this was not Geno's Island. To reach Vanuvia we had to travel by boat across the ocean.

We were all starting to regret the decision. Hailey got seasick and spent most of her time leaning over the side feeding the fish. Finally, we saw land and it was a welcome sight indeed.

On arrival to the island, Geno's schedule was so busy that we hardly had time to talk about what was happening. As soon as we landed, we were greeted with a huge ceremony. People were bowing before Geno calling him. "Ariihau Haunui," over and over.

Hailey and I were torn. Can we be heartbroken and happy for Geno at the same time? Will we lose our beautiful son to all of this ceremony and grandeur? Then again, even if he wanted to go home, could we in good conscience take him away from his homeland? Would they let us leave with our son?

Geno looked at us and mouthed the words, "Mom, dad?" and shrugged his shoulders.

I asked one of the men who brought us there, "Is my son safe?"

He smiled, "He couldn't be safer. The people will love him."

I asked, "What if he decides to leave and go back home?"

The man thought for a moment and then said, "Then, he will have two homes."

Hailey and I felt relieved, so we let our guard down to enjoy the moment with Geno. We could see that he was both elated and confused. Imagine, he had thought all of his life that he was nothing but street trash and here he was royalty the whole time.

We visited every site on the island. It was a small island. We hiked a lot and rode horses and there was a special car just for dignitaries. We all squeezed into the car with Geno and a couple leaders.

After a couple days, we got to spend an evening alone with just us family.

I asked, "Geno, what do you think of all of this?"

"It's a lot to process, dad. I don't know what to think. I mean, almost everything a person could want is at my fingertips, but it's not New York. I even had a couple of pretty girls ask me to marry them."

Hailey asked, "How did your dad and I miss that?"

Geno laughed, "Mom, these people are very clever. I noticed them distracting y'all several times to say things to me that they didn't want you to hear. One time they even told me that I don't have to go back home with you and dad, and that, if I want, I can stay here. The one guy said, 'There's nothing your parents can do to stop you from doing what you want here.' I told him, 'You obviously don't know my parents'. Then they laughed like it was a joke. But after I thought about it for a while, I realized that it didn't feel like a joke."

I said to Geno, "It's a lot to take in for a fifteen-year-old."

He interrupted me, "Dad, I'll be sixteen in a couple weeks, remember? Anyway, I'm just about ready to go home, already. I miss home, school, my friends, and most of all spending time with my family. If, after I finish my education, I feel like coming back to visit, that would be cool. Dad, I'm good. I'm going to be a lawyer, not a king. It's just not my style."

Hailey said, "Son, you've got a style? When did that happen?" We all laughed, but we all agreed to catch the next flight home.

With my imagination set off by Geno's report of the sneaky way that the people were behaving behind Hailey's and my backs, I thought to myself, "Suppose they do try to take our son? Suppose they try to force him to be their king?"

ADOPTED

The next morning, we were called before the council. Council members and tribal chiefs all sat at a long table facing our little family as we walked in and sat at a smaller table. The atmosphere was tense as the head councilman spoke. "We understand that your family has arranged a flight to take our Ariihau Haunui back to New York?"

I have been in some tough litigations but I was stuck trying to figure out what they were going to say next. The silence of the pause was deafening. We were caught. I looked at Hailey as I was preparing my response to the council.

Suddenly I heard my son, Geno speak, "I just want to say, it's been fun meeting you all. But the truth of the matter is that you are all still strangers to me. As a matter of fact, I was a stranger to myself until I went to live with my parents. You would have never found me because I was running around as a Vietnamese orphan who nobody wanted. My parents, Rashawn and Hailey Wright, took me in and I became a part of a bigger family, the Wright family. They've taught me many things. I'm in a great school and I plan to go on to become a corporate lawyer like my dad. I am an American, and as an American I have freedom of choice. I choose the people who love me, and I choose to go home."

The head councilman, with an angry look on his face, raised his voice, "Ariihau, but they are not your parents. They are not even your people! Look at them--they are black people!"

Geno, knowing that I was about to say something, put his arm out to hold me back. Then Geno, with amazing calm, said, "I love my real name. Maybe I'll decide to get it changed when I get back to New York. Maybe my name will be Ariihau Haunui Wright, but everybody will still call me Geno. Let me tell you something about adoption. Many people are blessed to know and live with their parents. Some of us are abandoned for one reason or another. You can't choose who your birth child is, but in adoption you chose someone that you will bring home into your house as a full member of the family. Adoption is a side of human nature that is more than natural--it's amazingly supernatural. Adoption is done by people who are able to love like God loves.

I want to let you know that I am proud of my parents and I hope to be like them. I didn't know my real parents, but I have come to know that they had to flee for their lives from this place. Now, you are making us feel like our lives may be in danger. In the process of my parents adopting me, I adopted them. It's more than natural--it's supernatural--it's spiritual. Nothing can break this bond. Not your trickery, not your threats, not your intimidation. So just give it up and let us catch our plane."

Hailey and I were standing straight and tall and proud but our faces were covered in tears of joy. What we had just heard from our son could have moved a nation, but it did not move the council.

The leader spoke, "We've learned a lot from you, young Ariihau Haunui, but we are not willing to lose you. We have not decided what to do with your adopted parents, but you, you will stay here with us!"

They escorted us back to our accommodations.

ADOPTED

That night, I shook Hailey while I covered her mouth and shushed her, then, I did the same with Geno. I told them each to be quiet, leave our luggage, and only take what they absolutely needed. Then, we took all of our clothes out of our suitcases and stuffed our sheets to make it look like we were still in our beds. We took our phones, which did not work here anyway, and our wallets and passports, as we crept into the night.

Earlier, while the council was focused on convincing Geno to stay, I hired a guy with a small boat to take us to the main island where the plan was that we could hire a plane to take us to the Philippines.

When we got to the shore and Hailey saw the small boat, she started to pace in a circle. "Oh, heck no! This is way too small! I'm not getting on this boat!"

It took a minute of whispering, but Geno and I finally talked her into getting in the boat and we took off. It didn't take long to doubt our decision. The further out we got, the choppier the waves became, until huge waves started hitting the small craft. I asked the boatsman, who we decided to call Cy because we couldn't pronounce his real name, if he had ever done this before. He replied that he had done this trip many times, but tonight the ocean was unusually rough. Then, Cy confessed that he had not used this small boat before, but he had navigated the trip in a larger boat that he did not own. It turns out that he didn't want to cut the owner of the bigger boat in on the money, so he took this smaller boat. Hailey was too afraid to lean over the side of this small boat, so she just heaved in the boat and it splashed all over our feet.

With those waves, Hailey's puke was the least of our concerns. By the time the waves grew their highest, we were halfway to the big island and it made no sense to turn back. We resolved to just continue the trip and pray. Suddenly, a huge wave hit the tiny craft and flipped the boat, throwing us all into the ocean.

The force of the wave scattered us in different directions. So, we called out until we located each other and gathered together in as much of a circle as we could muster. We floated and began to swim. Fortunately, we were all strong swimmers, even Cy, as old as he was, and we all managed to stay afloat. I kept talking to keep everyone encouraged. We even sang songs until Hailey broke out into, "Wade in the water, wade in the water children, wade in the water. God's gonna trouble the water."

Geno looked over and said, "Really mom? Really?"

We all laughed and drew strength from being a family. Even Cy laughed with us. Then, I said, "You know what we haven't done up till now?"

"Hailey answered, "Pray. Right?"

I said, "Yes! You've got it. Shall I lead us?"

Geno replied, "Yes, dad, let's pray."

"Heavenly Father, You have been with us the whole time of our existence. You are with us even now. We ask that You give us strength and show each of us what we are to learn and how we are to grow from this experience." I paused, like we do as a family when we ask God something in prayer, to listen to His response.

Cy questioned, "Is that it, is that all you are going to ask your God?"

Geno replied, "No Cy. When dad asks God a question, we, then, listen for an answer. No matter what, even in His silence, God answers. In this case, God told me, 'Hold on! I will send you a sign. In that sign will be your rescue.'"

Just then, something hit Hailey just beneath the water, so hard that I saw it move her body. Immediately, I swam under to see what was in the water with us. It was a bull shark and it was circling! There were other bull sharks that just seemed to ignore us. But this one bull shark was getting aggressive. I surfaced and asked Cy to give me his knife.

It seemed to be focused on Hailey. It bumped her again and I went after it. First, I tried punching it in the nose, but that only made it switch its focus to me. That was just what I wanted. "Come on, you monster, I'm the one you want!" When it attacked me, I avoided its bite and stabbed it in the eye. Then, as it swam by me, I slashed its gills. I dug so deep into its side that the knife came out of my hand and started to sink into the darkness of the murky ocean.

The young bull shark panicked and swam away. The other sharks sensed blood in the water and chased after the injured young bull.

I went after our only weapon of defense. As the knife sank, it seemed just out of my reach, so I went deeper and deeper. It was almost in my grasp when I realized I had dived much deeper than I should have. I might not be able to get back to the surface. Desperately, I did giant strokes towards the surface but it just seemed too far. Air bubbles started leaving my lungs. I swallowed a big gulp of water and thought to myself, "Rashawn, this is it buddy. Was that your last breath?"

Suddenly I broke the surface of the ocean and somehow the water I had swallowed came out like a fountain and I was able to breath deep gulps of air. Cy looked at me, bewildered.

Hailey just smiled, looked up and said, "We thank you, Father, for Your goodness and mercy. We thank you for the strength You have given this family. We have learned today that we are stronger than we ever dreamed. We thank you for the sunrise..."

Suddenly, Hailey hesitated, and then she said, "And most of all we thank you for the boat I can see headed right towards us."

I shouted, "What boat"?

I spun around in the water. We all started shouting and splashing water in excitement as the boat moved slowly towards us. Then, it suddenly stopped. Two men started tugging at a huge net on the right side of the boat facing away from us. They were struggling to pull in a huge catch.

Geno said, "What are we waiting for? That's our sign! Swim!"

The men couldn't hear us. The ocean was too loud and they were focused on their catch. So, we started swimming towards them. We all swam as fast as we could. It was Cy who got to the boat first. As Cy started to climb on the boat, one of the men picked up a gun and shot at Cy.

ADOPTED

He barely missed him when Hailey shouted, "We are not pirates. We need your help."

The one man asked, "Are you Americans?"

"Yes" I said. "And I'll pay you to take us to the big island."

When the man heard that, he told his friend to help us aboard. The men explained that this was not their usual fishing route. But when they weren't catching fish, they decided to go further out. The fish led them to this very spot and they only stopped to bring in the net.

Miraculously, on the fishing boat, Hailey seasickness was cured. I was shocked that she walked around the boat like she was a seasoned sailor. When they gave us food and water, she even ate some ceviche, a raw fish salad called kinilaw, and she didn't puke once.

From the big island we got a flight to the Philippines where we got a flight all the way to New York. We all slept almost the whole 16 hours it took to fly from Manila to New York.

When we walked into our house, my dad and mom were waiting for us by the front door. They walked with us into our living room. There was a loud shout of "Welcome home," from Rennie, Will, Jeff, his fiancée, Tommy and Judy. They were all in our living room, waiting to see our faces. As tired as Hailey, Geno and I were, we looked at each other and laughed.

Geno was the first to say, "Family is everything, pop!"

Hailey nodded in agreement and I just smiled. We hadn't showered in a while but it didn't matter. Will and Rennie's kids and Tommy and Judy's kids filled the house with a joyful noise and lots of energy. It was like a big party. Everybody was talking at the same time and it got pretty loud.

Mom and Rennie had cooked all of our favorites. The family all sat in the living room as Geno told the story of our travel to, our time in, and our escape from, Vanuvia. The kids sat with their mouths open, listening as Geno talked about our boat capsizing in the middle of the ocean. The little ones were motionless when he talked about the sharks. At the end of his story, everyone started teasing Geno about being the prince of Brooklyn.

Suddenly, the front doorbell rang. My dad answered the door. He came back into the room leading two men dressed in black suits. Geno, Hailey and I looked up and it was two men from Vanuvia. Two of the council members had followed us back to New York and had come to our home.

They looked at us and said, "Somehow, we knew that the rumors of your death at sea were not true. We had to see for ourselves."

Then, they moved towards Geno but when they saw the family gather close to him, they stopped and bowed.

The whole family, especially the kids, all at the same time went, "Whoa!"

Geno calmly said, "Y'all need to get up. You're embarrassing me in front of my family. I'll never live this down."

Will and Rennie's daughter, Barbara, said laughingly, "Too late now, Geno. We're way past that now! You've entered family legend."

I asked, "What do you guys want with my son? He's made his decision."

Then Hailey turned into momma bear. Putting her arm on Geno's shoulder she said, "Yeah, and we literally went through hell and high water to honor Geno's decision. Now, you will, too!"

Geno was his usual, amazingly mature and calm self. He was very soft spoken as he said, "Look, guys, we came all the way out to your island to see if it would work for me. I just couldn't do it. This is my family and I choose family. Please go back and honor my privacy. I'm not coming back to Vanuvia."

The men watched as the family closed ranks around Geno even tighter. One of the men said, "Fair enough, Prince Ariihau Haunui. We will leave, but we will send an invitation every year to present to you the opportunity to come and assume your birthright as royal prince of Vanuvia."

Then, they bowed once more, turned, and walked out to their car. Some of the family rushed to the windows and watched them drive away.

Then all the kids started bowing to Geno, calling him the Prince of Brooklyn. Geno chased them around the house laughing. The adults sighed in relief that everything was back to normal again. I think that Hailey was happier that the kids didn't break anything, running around roughhousing. But she wouldn't have changed a thing.

CHARLES LEE KNUCKLES

Tommy and Judy

Judy and I were happy that our church in Loren, Virginia was beginning to grow. I loved preaching, teaching, and leading this wonderful congregation a lot more than being a lawyer. I thought the diversity of the church membership was wonderful. To me, it was a blessing to be able to preach the gospel to such an amazing diversity of people. Truly, small town diversity is a beautiful thing. Coming from a diverse family, I was more than prepared for this blessing of an extended diverse family.

There was a small church a couple of blocks from our church. It had a small congregation of two hundred members. They suffered a series of tragedies. First, their pastor died, and soon after, they lost their church because of a fire. They had an all-black membership with nowhere to go. I invited them to join us in our majority-white church congregation. At first, I thought my church would fire me and run me out of town. Something happened during a sermon series of Jesus' "Sermon on the Mount." Everyone in our church welcomed our new members. Most everyone already knew each other, anyway. A little bit of heaven came down here to earth.

During this transition, two older members of our congregation delighted me, in particular. New to the church, Mr. Jimmy, a gray-haired, older black man had amazing energy. Mr. Jimmy came to church three days a week. He was always early. He enjoyed setting up the chairs in Fellowship Hall for special events. Mr. Jimmy also loved to sing, and does he ever have a beautiful deep voice. Mr. Jimmy met Mr. Nolan, a gray-haired, older white man. Mr. Nolan and Mr. Jimmy were exactly alike in every aspect. Actually, Mr. Nolan would come to church the same three days a week as Mr. Jimmy. He would come early and help set up Fellowship Hall as well. And, he could really sing, too, but he was a tenor. Soon, the two men would meet in church during the week and practice songs together. Their practices were like private concerts for the church staff and me.

Church was more than just Sunday to Mr. Nolan and Mr. Jimmy. They sang with such harmony that I would be in my office with the door open so I could enjoy their songs. I talked the choir director into giving them a couple of duet spots during service. They were just that good. They looked and sounded like masculine angels coming down from heaven to bless our church. Every time these two gentlemen sang, the congregation would clap and shout "amen" and "hallelujah" for their worship songs. I looked at these men with great admiration.

Sometimes, while working alone, I would daydream. I would wonder if my brother and I, after growing old together, would be anything like Mr. Nolan and Mr. Jimmy. What would we be doing with our time? I wished that Rashawn and Hailey would move to Loren so I could see my brother more often.

ADOPTED

Adopted: Tommy and Judy

My wife, Judy, worked in town for the school district. In her spare time, she started volunteering at the Wright Plantation Orphanage for Girls. Judy, being a total math-whiz and known as being a "mathlete," started teaching math and entry-level computer coding at the Plantation. I was so proud of her. I did not know how she would adjust to moving from Brooklyn to small town, Loren, Virginia so well. She seemed to be doing just fine. She was always busy.

Because Judy was pregnant, I wanted her to sit around the house and take it easy. I even offered to hire a house cleaner. Needless to say, that offer was rejected. My wife was happy for us to do all of the cleaning and cooking together. It wasn't my idea of quality time but I could see her point of view. Judy was not the "take it easy" kind of woman. Rennie, Will's wife, was only too happy for her help at the orphanage but she refused to accept Judy as a volunteer. Rennie insisted on paying Judy a fair wage for her level of expertise. Rennie wouldn't hear of it when Judy tried to explain that we didn't need the money.

Judy would earn every penny of that money when she had to work with some of the troubled girls. They were tough. Judy told me the story of her encounter with Deidre, a tough, 9-year-old girl who was among five young girls rescued from one of the most notorious human trafficking rings. These monsters were trying to get a foothold in the Virginia Beach area. Through a series of raids, the police had rescued many young girls. A few of the girls had no family in America. The court sent many of those girls to Rennie's orphanage, the Wright Plantation.

After dinner one Wednesday night, I was struggling with writing my sermon for Sunday. Suddenly, Judy walked into my office. Very rarely does my wife interrupt me when I'm working at home. This was a pleasant surprise. Judy invited me to come over with her and sit on the floor in front of the fireplace. Her timing was perfect. I was right in the middle of writer's block. I appreciated that a distraction was just what I needed. Also, I love talking to my wife, so she didn't have to ask me twice.

Judy led me by my hand to the thick, comfy rug. The fire was warm and inviting. The wood in the fire was crackling and it made me think of camping in the woods, except we were a lot more comfortable. We used a long pillow from the loveseat that we could share, to rest our heads. As we lay there, the fire radiated a soothing warmth. At first, we were just laying back, looking up at the ceiling, just relaxing. Then, Judy let out a quiet sigh and turned her head towards me.

She began by telling me, "When I first took the job with Rennie, I thought it would be just something casual to occupy my free time while you were at church. Well, Tommy, I've got to tell you, this job has been chocked full of challenges and adventures. This ministry is very rewarding. I knew I had to do something with my time or go crazy. I wasn't sure that this was it, because, as you know Tommy, I am a card-carrying introvert except when at work. Math is so much more reliable than people. People are your thing, not mine. Along the way, Rennie and I have become close friends. After a little people-skill coaching from Rennie, I started to get better at connecting with the girls. I began to see the importance of what I was asked to do. Most of these girls come from rough backgrounds. For many, first, they were failed by the people who were supposed to care for them, and then, they were failed by the system. Even now, some of the girls see what we are trying to do at the orphanage as just another part of the system that has failed them in the first place. Because of repeated disappointments, they can't see the possibilities right in front of them. I knew right away that unless I could show them the importance of math and computers, I would lose control of my class. This point was made crystal clear when I met a student named Deidre.

"It appears that a trafficking ring or somebody in a gang had taken Deidre from her family. She was taken so early in life that she doesn't even know her parents. She doesn't know where she was born. Rennie thought that Deidre was probably a Hispanic and European mix. She has bronze-colored skin, jet black hair, and piercing, blue eyes.

One day, I made the mistake of calling on Deidre to review an equation that I had just talked about. As a matter of fact, it was still written out on the dry-erase board. All Diedre had to do was to walk through what she had just heard and seen. Instead, Deidre disrupted the class by clowning me. In a sing-song kind of way, she made a string of derogatory comments about the way that I spoke. She mocked the fact that I used proper English. She went on to undermine all of my subsequent efforts to keep the class in order. Thanks to Deidre, it seemed like the whole class became out of control and they were throwing paper wads, running around, yelling, and laughing out loud. That is, until Rennie walked into the room. As soon as everyone saw her, they all sat down and got quiet. Tommy, I cannot tell you how defeated I felt that day. I felt like I was a student in front of my students because Rennie had to take control. That did not feel good."

I felt so bad for my wife that I stopped her right there. Brushing her hair back with my fingers, I said, "Aww honey..."

Judy stopped me in midsentence, and pushed my hands away, "Not you, too! Don't 'Aww, honey' me! Let me finish the story and don't treat me like a rookie. Anyway, that was my first disagreement with Rennie.

"After class, I went to her office and told her, 'Rennie I don't want to seem ungrateful but please keep out of my class and let me resolve my own issues.' Rennie responded, 'Alright, now, girl, that's the fire I like to see. You've got this.' 'Yes, I do got this,' I said, as I smiled and hugged her.

ADOPTED

"When I walked back to the classroom, there was Miss Deidre, alone, waiting for her showdown with me. She stepped towards me and had the nerve to get up close in my face. I guess she thought that she had to call me out, 'Oh, so you think that you can clown me in front of the class and show me up? Are you trying to make me look dumb?' She got closer, like she was about to get physical.

"I remained calm, after all she's a nine-year-old, right? I replied, 'No, Deidre, just the opposite. I was trying to show you that you are smart. I was trying to show you that I see you. I've noticed your work. You are just a step away from nailing this formula. Or maybe you already know it.'

"I could see her, calling on her resolve. 'Look, Teach, if you pull that little stunt of calling me out again, the only thing that's going to get nailed is you.'

"I could see the desperation in her face. 'Deidre, how far in life do you think that violence will get you. Now, I forgive you because I love you. We can move on, forget this little episode and try a do-over.'

"I could see a hurt look in Deidre's face. I knew then that I had said something that triggered her. It seemed that she was close to a breakdown, 'Oh, you're some kind of freak and you love me, huh? Just how attracted to me are you, Teach, huh? Am I sexy to you?'

"'Deidre, you've got it all wrong. The only person that I love like that is my husband. I'm talking about the love like Christ's love for us all. God loves you and He commands me to love you, too. Deidre, I'm not willing to give up on you. I'm going to keep testing you in math until you realize what I already know. You're a smart girl.'"

I was really feeling the emotion in Judy's story by now, so much so that I interrupted and blurted, "What happened next? Did she get angrier. Did she try to lay hands on you? Did you have to restrain her?"

Judy gave me that look that said, "hold your horses, mister". "No, dear, none of that happened. Diedre simply laid her head on my shoulder and cried a deep cleansing cry. I let her get it all out. It was then that I told her that I understood why she disrupted the class. I came to the conclusion that she was only trying to clown me because she thought I was trying to clown her by asking her a question about the equation. As we sat together, I gave Deidre a tissue to wipe her eyes and blow her nose. When she had done that, she suddenly walked to the dry-erase board. She picked up a marker and wrote, '10 – 10 + x = 15 -10' and under that, 'x =15 -10' then 'x=5' finally she wrote, '10 + 5 =15'.

"I looked at the board for a second, and then looked at Deidre. I gave her a smile and said, 'I knew it. For a 5th grader, that's pretty darn good.' She asked, 'How did you know that I was paying attention, Teach?'

"I replied, 'You're not the first kid that I've met that tried to hide their intellect. When I was about your age, I did the same thing back in my old neighborhood. Probably for the same reasons. My husband, Tommy, or Pastor Wright to you, did the same thing because of where he lived. He, too, thought that he had to hide the fact that he had a knack for math.'

ADOPTED

"We laughed together. Deidre said, 'Let's not tell anybody that we're secret math nerds.'

"I looked her in the eyes and said, 'Deidre, this is way too important to remain a secret anymore. God made you a certain way for a reason, and to find out what that reason is, you've got to be who you are! No more hiding. I see you, young lady. Let your light shine and let it take you all the way to the top. Don't be afraid anymore. I promise that I'll be right by your side.'"

I stopped Judy once more, and said, "Honey, that sounds like a serious commitment. How far are you willing to take it?"

Judy gave me that smile that means something is cooking in that big brain of hers. She looked deep into my eyes and said, "I've always loved it when you call me, honey. Brace yourself, Tommy. I'm willing to take this commitment all the way. I want to adopt Deidre."

We stayed up late into the night praying for God's guidance. Judy's prayers were so passionate that I wanted what she wanted. Even though Judy had only known Deidre for a few weeks, and I didn't really know her at all, we decided to start the adoption process for Deidre the next morning.

One of Rennie's caseworkers was in her office when Judy knocked on her door and entered. They were in a conversation about sending Deidre and another young girl, named Lynn, to a temporary foster home.

The caseworker went on to say, "Ms. Rennie, this foster home takes kids on a temporary basis. The foster home sits on a remote property and they operate like a bootcamp. They homeschool. There are four kids there, right now, but their capacity is six. We, on the other hand, have a waiting list that at the moment doesn't seem to be moving." She went on to say, "Quite frankly, Deidre and Lynn have been real challenges. Maybe a little tough-love might be just the thing that they need?"

That's when Judy interrupted, "You can forget about sending Deidre to that home. Tommy and I want to adopt her to our home. Rennie, can you ask one of your case workers to get the paperwork started?"

Rennie turned, "Judy, are you and Tommy sure about this?"

Judy smiled and said, "Rennie, we couldn't be any surer."

Even though I was proud of my wife, I wasn't as sure as she was about this decision. Judy had a bun in the oven, as the saying goes. So, we were pregnant, and we were adopting a nine-year-old little girl with big issues. But I'm on team-Judy. I'd support my wife through thick and thin. I was in!

Within a week, Judy brought Deidre home for the home trials. I watched as the young girl's eyes tried to take it all in. I guess it could be a lot. We have a large house with back decks and a rather large pool. I can't imagine how hard it must have been to process that this was where she would live now.

Until then it had been just Judy and I in the house. We spent all the time we could together. Now, Judy and Deidra spent so much time bonding that, I'm ashamed that I have to admit, I became a little jealous that the little one was receiving so much of my wife's attention. At times it seemed like I was left out of everything or was just the third wheel

ADOPTED

on a date. Looking back, I can't believe that I, a pastor of a church, was still so emotionally immature. But I was.

At some point, I realized that Deidre was intimidated by my presence because of what she had experienced while being trafficked by evil men. I was infuriated at those men. At the same time, I gained the deepest compassion for the little one. I knew that for a time, until she got to know me, I would have to walk on eggshells around Deidre. Judy would give me progress reports at bedtime. The things that she revealed to Judy were enough to make a grown man cry. Those early days I was in an emotional whirlwind. So, I called Will and Jeff.

Will and Jeff came over for lunch. We sat outside by the grill and talked. I told them all what my new daughter was going through.

Will said, "That must be a tough one. How are you doing with this, Tommy?" I guess, it was evident that I was angry.

I said, "I want to go there and bust up that trafficking ring."

Jeff stood up and put his hand out in a stop signal, "Whoa, Lone Ranger! That's way too big of job, even for the three of us."

Then Will spoke. "I have a buddy, his name is John House. He is a detective with the Field Intelligence Unit of the Virginia State Police. Get all the information that you can from your daughter--descriptions, locations and most importantly, names. My buddy John will get the job done. The police want to put these guys out of business. They just need information. Your daughter won't have to worry anymore."

We all took the rest of the day off from work and jumped in the pool.

I told Judy what I had done and I thought that she would be happy. Boy, was I wrong. She went into the play room and told Deidre that we had to go out for a moment. Then, she directed me to get into the car.

We rode down the road just out of sight of the house and she started yelling at me as loud as she could. "What do you mean by doing this without consulting me? Do you know how traumatic that kind of interview would be for Deidre?"

I suggested that we get out of the car. When we did, I walked around the car and gave her a gentle hug.

I said, "Look honey, I'm not suggesting that anybody interview Deidre. I am suggesting that she have these talks with you, just the two of you alone. I don't think that this will interrupt the bonding process that you are developing. Am I wrong? If you still think that I am out of line, I will stop the project. I think that what's important is that with that information, we can get these monsters off the streets. You can let Deidre know that her identity will always be protected. Plus, when the adoption process is complete, she'll have a new name."

Judy melted into my arms and said, "I'm sorry that I exploded. I know that this is the right thing to do. Besides, I've got a lot of that information already. It's going to be delicate, but I'll get names, descriptions, and locations for the detectives as well."

We kissed and got back into the car to drive back home. When we got home, Deidre was in the pool, swimming laps.

We both looked and smiled, then Judy got into her swimsuit and jumped in the pool. From inside the kitchen, I watched them laughingly race each other for a second, then I went to my study to write Sunday's sermon.

One week later, after our prayer time, right before I turned out the lights, Judy suggested that I look at my emails. She had sent me all the information that the detectives request. It seems that Deidre felt safe enough in her new home and was happy to help. Judy and Deidre had gone over maps and found addresses of the operation. Deidre even remembered landmarks around the house of the big boss well enough to identify his address. I forwarded the information to Detective John House. It wasn't long before they confirmed the intel and coordinated their raids with the State Police Tactical Team and SWAT. With the help of our brave little girl, they ended up taking down a whole trafficking cartel.

In the privacy of our home, I started calling Deidre, "The biggest little hero the world would never know." She warmed up to me.

One day, Deidre ran into my study and said, "Dad, mom's ready to go to the hospital. My baby sister is ready for birth!"

We didn't wait for the ambulance. I grabbed Judy's "go bag," helped her to the car, and off we drove.

Deidre and I stood together holding hands in the delivery room, as we watched baby Susan Christina enter the world. We sat with Judy and baby Susan for a long time. Deidre and I took a walk to get some food.

CHARLES LEE KNUCKLES

I asked, "Deidre, remember when the birth of your little sister started? When you ran into my office, did you mean it when you called me Dad?"

Deidre turned away and spoke, "Is that going to be, okay? Are you going to be my dad?"

"Sweetheart, I've been your dad since the day you came home."

Deidre turned to face me, "Okay, yeah, I meant it, dad!" She gave me the biggest hug.

We stayed overnight in Judy's room. Two days later, we happily took all of our family home.

Judy and I gave birth to one more sweet, precious little girl, who we named Gianna. Who knew that I would find so much delight in being a girl-dad. But I **was** hopelessly out numbered in our immediate family. So, I would hang out with Jeff and Will. When the girls all got together and went on their field trips, we boys would find camaraderie, hanging out by my pool. We didn't smoke cigars or drink beer, but we would eat bad food, belch, and occasionally, fart. Will and I did not cuss but sometimes Jeff would include a cuss word in the conversations and we all would laugh. We didn't just do competitive papa-bear stuff around the pool, sometimes we would go hiking, camping, hunting or fishing. We worked hard and we played hard. We were just three brothers enjoying life. The fact that we could be ourselves around each other felt rather freeing.

However, I did miss my brother Rashawn. I called him as often as I could. Sometimes our days were so busy that we wouldn't be able to talk until the middle of the night.

ADOPTED

Rashawn and Geno were close but I wished that he and Geno could be with us, enjoying the adventures with Will, Jeff and me.

One Sunday, after the church service was finished, I noticed a lady was still in the back of the church. She was looking down as if she was praying. The ushers were careful not to disturb the lady. They skirted around her as they politely did their cleaning. Mr. Jimmy and Mr. Nolan were usually in the back pews talking and laughing together, but even they were being as quiet as possible. The young lady continued to stay in her seat long after everyone else had left.

I walked over to her, and asked, "Can I sit?"

The lady was sobbing into her hands. Without looking up at me, she shook her head yes, indicating that I could sit with her.

I sat down, and I asked, "Would you like for me to pray with you?"

She would not look at me but I heard her muffled answer, "Yes, please Pastor."

I asked, "What is your name, young lady?"

With her head still hung, she replied, "My name is Robin, sir."

I was suspicious from the way her speech was muffled. It felt like something was very wrong. "Robin, everything is going to be alright. You are safe, my child. Can you look at me please?"

Robin finally lifted her head, and her eyes met mine. Tears began to flow not just from her eyes but from of my eyes as well. There were big lumps on her forehead, her eyes were blackened. There was dried blood encrusted around her lips. They were bloody and swollen. Robin's whole face was swollen from a horrible beating, and it seemed like her jaw might have been broken. Immediately, I said, "I'm calling an ambulance; you need medical assistance."

Robin went into a panic, "No cops please. I'll get into more trouble. I don't want to get him mad at me. He'll kill me!"

I held her to my chest, "May the peace of Christ be with you, dear daughter. You are safe in this church."

In my arms, Robin's trembling ceased, and she did seem to be at peace. There was one last deacon in the back of the church. I gave her a cue and she made the call to emergency services.

I asked Robin, "Who was it that did this to you, my dear?"

She answered with a name I had not heard in years. "My boyfriend, Q."

I knew Quinton from years earlier. For a short time, we lived in the orphanage together. He and his friend Todd was at the Farm the same time that Rashawn and I were there. I knew that hearing his name meant trouble. But if I had anything to do with it, this man Q, from this moment forward, would never again lay a hand on Robin.

The ambulance came to take Robin. I let her know that I would follow it to the hospital. I had to give a report to the police. They were already aware of Quinton and his band of thugs. Quinton's group already had charges pending against them. But the authorities had not been able to find Q or his gang's hideout. Now, there were new charges added to Q's list. I would do everything in my power to make sure these charges would stick.

I knew that the aid that I gave to Q's girlfriend, Robin, would put my family in jeopardy. So, I called home and told Judy of the danger and that she and the girls should immediately move to the Farm for safety. Things were on high alert. Now, I really wished Rashawn was with me.

Sure enough, somehow Q found out that Robin had come to the church. He also found out that it was me that had called emergency services to aid her, and that I had called the police. I don't know how he knew where I lived. I chalk it up to it being in a small town where everybody knows everything. Just as I had anticipated, he and his gang broke into my house and tried to wreck it. They broke windows and furniture. Fortunately, my wife and children were safe, and fortunately, my alarms scared them off. Still, Q was sending me a very clear message. Later, he even went to the hospital to kidnap Robin, but we had already moved her to different hospital. He and his gang were almost captured at the hospital but they were too many and moved too fast for the few hospital guards.

The next Sunday, after church and after all the congregation had left, when it was just me and a couple of deacons cleaning up, it happened. Three vehicles stormed into the church parking lot. I guess deep down I knew it would happen, but I naively thought that even Q would have respect for the sanctity of the church.

It went like clockwork. It was like a paramilitary group making a planned and coordinated attack. With weapons drawn, they rushed in the church door. Two had pistols, one, a shotgun. The men subdued the ushers. Q and two of his men walked into the church behind his attack force.

He marched right up to me. The largest of the men held my arms while Q punched me in the gut. I folded over and threw up a little. He held my head up, looked me in the eyes with a menacing stare and said, "Remember me, Little Tommy?" Then he laughed and punched me in the face. I was half conscious when I heard him say, "You've been sticking your nose in where it doesn't belong, Little Tommy. Now, I'm going to have to hurt you."

I said, "Look Q, you've got me, let the ushers go."

Q just laughed. Then one of the ushers set off the church alarm and ran. One of Q's guys took a couple shots at him but he got away.

Q started yelling, "We've got to get out of here! Let's take Little Tommy where I can take my time with him."

They dragged me out of the church to a van and threw me in the back. That was the last thing that I remember. I blacked out.

ADOPTED

Rashawn

Tommy's return to pastor the church infuriated the man called Q, who was once a boy named Quinton in the orphanage at the Farm with us. Q was still hanging out with Loki, another boy from the Farm, whose real name was Todd. Tommy pointed them out to Will because they were organizing a white supremacist gang on the Farm. Now they were fully organized and very dangerous. Because my brother had helped a woman Q was abusing, they kidnapped Tommy and probably would kill him.

They secretly followed Tommy until one day they caught him in the church and blitzed ambushed him. Q and his men overpowered Tommy and threw him into a van. One of the ushers pulled the church alarm. Another usher was upstairs in the church. She was looking out of the window and saw everything. She saw her pastor disappear into the van. She called the police and gave them a description of the van. Deacon Rice, who had pulled the fire alarm, was able to run out of the back door and into the woods. He avoided getting shot and was able to tell the whole story.

The police contacted Judy, Tommy's wife, who in turn contacted my dad. We were all on a plane headed back to Virginia in no time. As mom, dad, Geno and I sat on the plane, we prayed for Tommy's safe keeping. We prayed, using Psalm 59, that God would protect Tommy from his enemies.

But Tommy wasn't safe in the hands of Q and Loki. We found out later that they enjoyed beating and torturing my brother. In their sick, twisted minds, they were having fun.

As soon as I got to the Farm, I went to Tommy's church. I called a congregational meeting. Although Tommy had introduced us as his family to the church, my color still seemed to surprise them. It took some adjustment for them to see me in a role of leadership. I said, "If anyone of you know where my brother is being held, you've got to speak up."

No one said anything. I got the sense that they were all afraid. I figured if I let people approach me alone, they might feel free to talk. "I'll be in my brother's office going through his documents, if anyone wants to talk."

Later that evening, there was a knock on the door. It was Richie, the boy we had saved after he had tried to push Tommy into the river.

"Richie, have you come to pray with me about Pastor Tommy?"

"No Rashawn. I know where Tommy is right now."

"Where is he, Richie?"

"You remember Q and Loki?"

"Yes! Where do they have him?"

ADOPTED

"He is at the old tire warehouse."

I knew the place. I then gave Richie my dad's card, "Here's a number Richie, call my dad. He is with my brother in-law Will. Tell them where to meet me."

I got into my car and sped to my brother's side. I didn't even stop to think, because I knew time was of the essence.

When I got to the warehouse, I could see lights, so I knew people were in there but I didn't know how many. I found the perfect piece of wood to use as a club. It was an old table leg. I quietly crept up to sneak a peek into a dirty window at the back of the building. I saw my brother Tommy tied up in a chair. His head was slumped over. He was a bloody mess.

There were two men there. I recognized them as Q and Loki. I tried the back door--it wasn't even locked. They must have felt pretty secure. I took a deep breath and I charged the two men, striking Loki first with the club. Loki fell to his knees. I didn't know if he was dead or not but I didn't care.

Q made a lunge for a pistol but I dove on him before he could aim it at me. A shot fired. Loki screamed. Q had shot Loki by accident. With one hand on the gun and the other keeping Q's other hand from punching me, I head-butted him, and blood squirted from his nose. Then I head-butted him again. Down went Q with me on top. I took the gun from his hand and smacked him silly with it.

Two of his friends heard the commotion and rushed in from the front but when they saw the pistol in my hand, they ran back out the room. Q was knocked out, and I think the other men were planning an attack.

CHARLES LEE KNUCKLES

I went to my brother and untied him. I got Tommy hunkered down behind a recliner. I checked the gun for how many bullets I had to defend us. It had only one bullet left. Just as I was trying to figure out how I was going to take those two guys out, Dad, Will and Jeff busted through the door with one of Q's men by the scruff of his neck.

Jeff said, "Wait here, Rashawn, the police are on their way."

I yelled back, "I'm not waiting."

I picked my brother Tommy up in my arms and ran to my car. I drove like a madman to the hospital and carried Tommy into the emergency room. They took him right into the ICU. Then, they cleaned me up with some butterfly stitches on my forehead. Those head-butts had left their marks.

After the police took my statement, we all, the whole family, sat in the lounge of the hospital waiting for news of my brother. We comforted Judy as much as possible. The doctors were not bringing us anything positive. Tommy was seriously hurt.

Finally, the doctor came in and said, "Mr. Wright is awake. He's a strong man to survive what he went through."

Dad asked, "Can we go in to see him?"

The doctor cautioned us, "You can go in for a little while but he needs to rest. How fast he recovers depends on his rest. The body heals itself through rest."

We all were filled with joy as Tommy looked up and said, "Family!"

I joked with him. I didn't know what to say. I was so happy that I said something stupid, of course. "Big bro, you've got to hurry up and get well, so you and Judy can challenge me and Hailey on the basketball court. We gonna school y'all."

Tommy smiled and said, "Lil' bro', you must have forgotten my wife's three-point game!"

We all laughed and probably made way too much noise. Every time we visited Tommy, the nurses had to shush us.

I knew that my brother would want his church to stay together so I led the next Sunday service. I preached on Paul's message on endurance, the first Sunday. I think the congregation was ok with my sermon. So, they invited me to do the next Sunday.

I was preaching from Acts 3 about the man who was lame from birth and sat and begged at the Beautiful Gate. I was describing how the man was sitting and begging and when he saw John and Peter just about to go into the Temple, he asked for alms. Right as I said that, I heard a voice coming from the back of the church. It was my brother Tommy, finishing my sermon.

Tommy, with a voice so strong the whole church turned, recited the scriptures from memory with each step he took. *"Peter said, 'Look at us.' So, he gave them his attention, expecting to receive something from them. Then Peter said, 'Silver and gold I do not have, but what I do have I give you: In the name of Jesus Christ of Nazareth, rise up and walk.' And he took him by the right hand and lifted him up, and immediately his feet and ankle bones received strength. So, he, leaping up, stood and walked and entered the temple with them—walking, leaping, and praising God. And all the people saw him walking and praising God. Then they knew that it was he who sat begging alms at the Beautiful Gate of the temple; and they were filled with wonder and amazement at what had happened to him."*

Tommy was stepping strong with a spiritual step. The whole church was so filled with joy that everyone stood up. We clapped in the rhythm of Tommy's steps as he preached and walked right up to the stage. As Tommy walked up the stairs of the stage, I was sobbing with joy. Then, my brother took me into his arms and we just hugged. One by one the whole family just embraced on the church stage, first, his wife Judy, who came in with him, then, Hailey, dad, mom, Geno, Rennie, Jeff, Will, his mom and dad, and his sister and brother. The congregation went wild. They all cheered and clapped for what seemed like forever. The sound echoed off the church walls, seemingly out into the whole community. Rennie led the entire congregation, chanting, "We are stronger than hate. We are stronger than hate..." on and on. The church did not tire out that day as we celebrated my brother's return.

Two weeks later, before returning to New York, I bought a house in Loren to spend more time with my brother. I'd had my eye on this house for a week. I had it checked out, and it was a winner. Dad wanted me to take over the firm, so I couldn't just leave New York. Imagine that, me, Rashawn Wright, the CEO of one of the most prestigious law firms in New York. My son, Geno, was my "Wright-hand" man! Get that play on words? Yeah, I know it's kind of corny, but I still like corny.

ADOPTED

    Fortunately, because of dad's hard work, and Geno being in New York, the firm was running so well that I could work remotely a lot more often. So, the whole family could fly to Loren for longer periods of time. Much to all of our surprise, upon dad's retirement, mom and dad decided to move to Loren. My parents kept the big house in New York for a long time. Mom and dad went to Tommy's church where they did a lot of volunteering. But most of their time was spent at the Wright Farm or at the Wright Plantation. They never ran out of things that they enjoyed doing. The whole Wright family had returned to the Wright Farm and the Wright Plantation. But this is not the end of the story.

Milton Keynes UK
Ingram Content Group UK Ltd.
UKHW022016240924
448733UK00016B/969